KU-796-201

White Fox is already a bestselling novel in China – and no wonder! Animals, adventure, magic and real heartfelt emotion: what's not to love? Join Dilah, our young fox hero, as he embarks on a dangerous quest to transform into a human being. By the end of this novel, I guarantee you'll be hungry for more of Chen Jiatong's totally unique and classic storytelling. Do you think the animal transformation happens the other way round too? If so, I would like to be the seal. You?

BARRY CUNNINGHAM
Publisher
Chicken House

WHITE FOX

Chen Jiatong

TRANSLATED BY JENNIFER FEELEY

2 PALMER STREET, FROME, SOMERSET BA11 1DS

Original Chinese text © Chen Jiatong 2014
English translation by Jennifer Feeley © Chicken House 2019
Cover and interior illustrations © Viola Wang 2019

Originally published in China as *Dilah and the Moonstone* by
People's Literature Publishing House in 2014
Currently published by Jieli Publishing House

First published in Great Britain in 2019
Chicken House
2 Palmer Street
Frome, BA11 1DS
www.chickenhousebooks.com

Chen Jiatong has asserted his right under the Copyright, Designs and
Patents Act 1988 to be identified as the author of this work.

All rights reserved.
No part of this publication may be reproduced or transmitted or utilized in
any form or by any means, electronic, mechanical, photocopying or
otherwise, without the prior permission of the publisher.

Cover and interior design by Steve Wells
Cover and interior illustrations by Viola Wang
Typeset by Dorchester Typesetting Group Ltd
Printed and bound in by CPI Group (UK) Ltd, Croydon CR0 4YY

The paper used in this Chicken House book is made
from wood grown in sustainable forests.

1 3 5 7 9 10 8 6 4 2

British Library Cataloguing in Publication data available.

ISBN 978-1-912626-08-3
eISBN 978-1-912626-49-6

CHAPTER 1

Secret Language and Legend

Faraway at the North Pole, the night was quiet and serene. A blue aurora of light flared to life against the black velvet sky, winding through the brilliant stars like a lithe, shimmering curtain. The vast snowfields and hills were waking from their deep slumber, a soft breeze stroking the drifting snow, swirling up the glittering crystals.

Beneath the thick snow, there was an underground den. The inside of the den was pitch-black, but the distinct sound of voices trickled out nonetheless.

'Mama!' a child called.

'What is it, darling?' the mother asked, smiling.

'I can't sleep.'

'You napped too long this afternoon, didn't you?' the mother gently teased.

'Mama, tell me a story. Can you tell me about Merla again?'

'You've heard that one so many times.'

'I still want to hear it!'

'OK, if you want to hear it, Mama will tell you,' the mother said lovingly. 'More than a thousand years ago, Merla was the Great Sage of the Arctic foxes. It's said that her entire body was covered in fiery red fur, which is extraordinarily rare for Arctic foxes . . .'

The little white fox listening to the story is the hero of our tale: Dilah. He was curled up against his mother's chest, tightly wrapped in her big tail, snug as a bug. He listened to his mother's story, the tip of his nose nudging her chin, feeling like the happiest little fox in the world.

Dilah's family den was buried deep beneath the snowfields of the Arctic Circle, soft hay strewn inside, making it feel warm and cosy. When Dilah's older brother Alsace turned one (the age when foxes become adults), he'd left home to join a skulk of Arctic foxes and live an independent life – that was before Dilah was even born. Now that five-month-old Dilah was the only cub, his parents focused all their love on him. At bedtime, he'd pester his mother to tell him stories, and during the day, he'd beg his father to give him piggyback rides. Young Dilah didn't seem to have a care in the world.

Dilah's family had moved three times since his birth. They kept moving from one hidden place to another, always avoiding contact with other animals. Strangely, no matter where they ended up, a few white foxes would always track them down. Each time, Papa would send Dilah away and talk to them in private. Growing up like this, Dilah hadn't made a single friend.

At the end of the snowfield, there was a small town called Lapula. The people who lived there were cut off from the rest of the world. In the northern part of town sat a small two-storey house, the red roof blanketed in thick snow, the chimney puffing black smoke toward the sky. The stone path from the front door had been recently cleared – both sides piled high with snow – and led straight to a white pine fence. A black van was parked in the yard, where several hardy pine trees grew.

Dilah often wandered near the house – a little closer every day. The morning after his mother's story, he watched as a man drove the van up to the gate as usual, the engine rumbling, the exhaust pipe spitting out smoke. Dilah came over to the fence by the house and sat on the snow, peering through the window as two children bounded down the stairs, the creaking of the wooden steps audible to his keen ears.

'Bella, your hat's on inside out!' the children's mother cried. She had curly blonde hair, Dilah noticed. 'And Peter, if you wear your scarf this way ever again, I promise I won't knit you a new one next winter! Now hurry up or you'll be late for school.'

Peter giggled and tied the scarf tightly over his mouth.

The woman opened the front door, Peter and Bella bouncing outside behind her. Peter had on thick blue gloves, a blue hat, a yellow scarf and a colourful fluffy coat. Bella carried a backpack and wore a heavy pink coat and tall white hat with a giant pom-pom on the tip. She looked like a snowman.

Though Papa had warned Dilah more than once to stay away from humans, a fierce curiosity glued him to the ground. He couldn't take his eyes off the house that puffed smoke, the car that made rumbling sounds, the colourful clothing . . . Humans were so fascinating!

'Get in the car, kids!' the man said, rolling down the window of the van.

The mother went over to the car and opened the door. 'Peter, try to pay attention in class. Your teacher has complained to me several times!'

'Yes, Mum,' Peter said impatiently, trudging over to the car door.

'Oh! Peter, hurry – look quickly!' Bella

exclaimed, her little finger pointing at the fence.

Peter gazed beyond the yard. 'Wow!'

Dilah was frightened but thrilled. He stayed perfectly still, his heart beating terribly fast. He was perched on the ground like some sort of magical snow creature: a pair of bright and piercing black eyes, two small round ears, and a large bushy tail trailing behind, his pure-white body nearly blending in with the snow.

'It's so beautiful!' the woman sighed.

'What is it?' The man stuck his head out the car window, straining to catch a glimpse of Dilah, his entire face turning red from the cold. 'Oh, an Arctic fox . . . you don't see those too often.'

Bella gave Dilah a friendly wave, and Peter whistled. Dilah cocked his head, curious.

'OK, kids. You're really going to be late, now. Get in the car!' the woman urged, looking at her watch.

'But Mum,' Bella said softly, 'can't we—'

'Perhaps you'll have another chance later,' the woman said, smiling. 'Maybe our little friend will be back.' She picked up Bella and kissed her, then gave Peter a peck on the forehead. Peter seemed like he was about to protest.

'Bye!' Bella called to Dilah in a sweet voice, hopping in the car and waving again. Peter climbed awkwardly in after her.

'Say goodbye to Mum,' the man said.

'Bye, Mum.'

'See you tonight,' replied the woman, wrapping her coat around her body.

The car and the roar of its engine faded away. The woman watched as it grew smaller and smaller, then suddenly remembered the small white fox. Turning around, she found there was no sign of him, only a trail of clover-shaped paw prints left behind in the snow.

From then on, Dilah was like a bee drawn to a flower – he couldn't help but sneak over to the house and quietly study the family, spying on their happy life, and never telling his parents. Sometimes the children noticed Dilah. Bella always made a fuss and called for her mother to come watch with her, while Peter would tiptoe over to the fence alone and extend a friendly hand. The children even worried that Dilah might freeze when it got especially cold, and wanted to dress him in their own hats and scarves. But because of Papa's warning, Dilah never let the children get too close.

Dilah thought about the family day and night, longing to be human. He dreamt about how wonderful it would be if he, his father, and mother could become humans, live in a house that puffed smoke, ride in a car that made rumbling sounds and wear colourful clothing . . . what a rich and varied life! If they were human, he was sure they wouldn't have to move around so much. Humans were the kings of the animals: they were never afraid.

One evening, as the sun was setting, the western horizon aglow and casting blood-red light on to the snowfields, steaming white smoke billowed from the chimney of the small house. Dilah sat close to the fence surrounding the garden, fascinated as always by the movements of the humans inside. It wasn't until the family drew the curtains that Dilah realized just how late it was getting – he turned tail and headed home, knowing his parents would be worried.

He hurried back to the den, only to discover that his parents were nowhere to be found. They must've gone to catch lemmings. He crouched just inside the mouth of the den, looking out, patiently waiting, his stomach growling with hunger.

The dark night unfurled its wings, sparkling stars slowly climbing up the evening sky. Mama and Papa still hadn't come back, and Dilah was growing restless – today's food must've been hard to find. Just then, he heard heavy wheezing and saw a shape approaching through the gloom. Dilah leapt out of the hole in the snow to greet his parents as they returned from the hunt, but the shocking sight that awaited him would haunt him for many nights to come.

His mama was struggling to reach the entrance to the den, her stomach streaked with blood. Dilah drew in a deep, cool breath. What was going on?

'Mama, what is it? Where's Papa?' Dilah

looked at his mother with watery eyes.

'Your father – he . . .' She hesitated.

'What happened to him?' Dilah asked, his voice cracking.

Avoiding Dilah's gaze, she staggered back into the den and collapsed on the hay, her entire body shaking uncontrollably.

'Mama . . . what happened?' Dilah couldn't bring himself to think about it – hoping his imagination was far worse than the truth.

Outside the den, the sky darkened, and the cold wind began to shriek.

'Dilah, we came across a human . . .'

'Human?' Dilah's head jerked up at the almost forbidden word.

'Yes, a hunter,' his mother said sadly. A gust of bitterly cold wind blew into the cave. Dilah's back was freezing, his chest suddenly tight. *Hunter.* The word left a scar on his heart.

'We were looking for food on the beach. Who'd have thought a hunter would be there?' His mother choked up, and could only speak between rasping breaths. 'He raised his shot-gun at us. We ran off immediately, but your papa . . . he was shot . . . I'm hurt too . . .'

'Is Papa coming back?' Dilah's tears rushed out. He felt lost.

Sobbing, his mother said nothing. Dilah was overcome with despair. His father was dead. Never again would he take him to look for food, never again would he protect him, never again would he give him a piggyback ride. The wind outside the den howled even more mournfully. A scattering of snowflakes floated in the air. A blizzard was coming.

'Dilah, my darling, my time is running out. There's something I must tell you. Whether you succeed is up to you,' Mama said, clearly fighting to suppress the pain in her stomach.

'No, Mama! You'll get better soon.' Dilah tried to comfort her. Her weak voice made his heart sink. 'When you're better, I'll bring you out to rest in the sun!'

'I'm like the snow outside: by the time sunlight arrives, I'll be gone.'

'Mama, don't talk like that!' His eyes welled up with tears. Trying not to let them fall, he nudged his mother with the top of his head.

'Dilah, do you know the difference between humans and animals?' Mama asked.

He felt suddenly guilty. *Humans*. That word again. 'I . . .'

'Humans are the masters of this world – they do whatever they please and enjoy all kinds of privileges. An animal, however, must endure a lot,' she whispered, her voice trembling. 'In nature, the weak are the prey of the strong, cruel and dangerous. We live in a constant state of fear. And our fates are firmly in the hands of humans, like your papa and me . . . never able to escape . . .'

Dilah gave his mother a strange look. He couldn't stop thinking about the family he'd been watching for the past few weeks. They seemed so friendly, so warm . . . yet now he had no choice but to accept the fact that a human had destroyed *his* happy little family and robbed him of his father . . . and perhaps his mother too.

'But there is one thing you should know.' His mother's voice turned serious, her every word carved deep in Dilah's heart. 'Listen, my child: there's a way to change our destiny. Legend has it that the patron saint of the Arctic foxes, Ulla, created a secret treasure like no other. It contains an incredible magic that can turn animals into humans!' She took a deep, painful breath, watching Dilah closely. 'Tell Mama – would you like to become human?'

Suddenly, Dilah pushed the human family from his mind. How could he have spent all his time watching them, instead of appreciating his own family? 'No, I don't want anything, I just want you to get better, Mama.'

'I know that's not true. I've seen you, Dilah. You've been watching that house on the edge of town.'

His eyes widened. 'But . . .'

'Yes, we've known all along. We saw you return to that family, day after day. Don't worry, little one. All animals dream of becoming human.' She looked at her son affectionately. 'I know you long for it too. And that's all right. Don't hate all humans because of what happened to us. There are both good and evil humans: you need to see that for yourself.'

'M-hm . . .' Dilah nodded, struggling not to cry.

'There's something hidden beneath the dirt in the deepest part of our den that can lead you to Ulla's secret treasure, but you must be careful – don't let anyone else know this secret, especially other foxes!' She struggled to enunciate each word. 'Guard it with your life. Remember, when you've given up all hope, you can turn to our patron saint Ulla for guidance.'

'I'll remember . . .' Dilah trailed off, his throat thick with tears.

'Promise Mama you'll take good care of yourself. Mama will always love you. I'm a bit sleepy, and want to rest for a while . . .'

'Mama, don't sleep, OK? Tell me another story,' Dilah pleaded. He wasn't ready to let go, not yet.

'OK, Mama will tell you another story, one I know you've never heard. This one's about two great heroes among us Arctic foxes: the story of Gale and Blizzard.' She narrowed her eyes at Dilah, as if she were trying hard to focus. She smiled, but her voice was weak when she started to speak again. 'A few years ago, the patriarch of the white foxes, Nicholas, declared war on the blue foxes in a dispute over territory.

'The war continued for two years. Finally, the key battle was set to take place – and the blue foxes had the upper hand. We white foxes came up with a plan, but it was a dangerous mission. When no one else was willing to fight, two sworn brothers heroically stepped forward. They used their own lives as bait to distract the blue foxes' forces. They defeated twelve seasoned blue fox fighters, but it was all so that Nicholas could raid the enemy camp, winning the war and saving the entire fox troop. The story of the two spread throughout the Arctic. In awe, the blue foxes renamed them Gale and Blizzard.' Her breathing grew lighter and lighter, her expression completely serene. 'The two of them made the enemy tremble with fear, especially Blizzard. He was strong . . . brave . . . calm . . . Mama will always remember his . . . charming . . . smile . . .' Her eyes glistened with tears and fluttered shut.

'Mama, don't fall asleep – look at me! Tell

me another story!' Dilah gently nosed his mother, his heart filling with grief when she didn't raise her head.

'I'm begging you, Mama, open your eyes . . .' He pushed her again, tears streaming down his face. But she was gone.

Dilah felt as if his world had suddenly crumbled, and everything before him had faded. Mama had left him for ever – never again would they play-fight, never again would she tell him a story, never again would she wrap him up in her big tail and kiss him.

'Mama . . .' Dilah sat beside his mother and sobbed. 'What should I do?'

Over the course of one evening, Dilah went from being the happiest little fox in the world to an orphan. His heart was empty. His future seemed empty too. He curled up in his mother's tail, helplessly nestling up against her. He wept until he was completely exhausted, then fell asleep in a daze . . .

'Mama, wake up!'

The next morning, Dilah nudged his mother

with a small furry paw, but she remained still and cold as ice. He hadn't wanted to believe that she was truly gone. His heart ached, and his eyes were blurry with tears. He spent the morning burying her, sorry that he couldn't lay his father alongside her.

Afterwards, heart heavy, he dragged his worn-out body back into the den. *There's something hidden beneath the dirt in the deepest part of our den that can lead you to Ulla's secret treasure*, his mother had said. Reluctantly, he started to dig, and at last unearthed a parcel. It was tightly wrapped in yellow leather, and there was something hard inside. It was the only thing his mother had left for him. He was curious, but wasn't ready to open it yet.

Dilah looked around at the small den he had shared with his parents. Only yesterday, he had felt so safe here, but he didn't feel that way any more. It no longer felt like home. Besides, his mother had told him to take the package and follow his dream of becoming human.

Dilah wiped away his tears, gripped the parcel between his teeth, and flew out of the den like an arrow, never looking back.

The blizzard raged. The sky was pitch-dark, a fierce wind sweeping up the heavy snow and beating the ground. A small, frail white fox dashed through the whistling flurries. Dilah gasped and panted heavily, clutching the small yellow package in his mouth, trying to forget the sorrow of losing his parents.

Eventually, he slowed down, shaking the snow from his body. Although he was carrying the parcel, he didn't feel drawn in any particular direction. Was it guiding him to Ulla's secret treasure, as his mother had promised? 'Mama . . .' He gazed up at the sky in confusion. It was as if he could make out his mother's loving smile among the cluster of dark clouds.

He ran and ran, losing track of time. After a while, he recognized a jagged, icy canyon plunging through the landscape. Dilah's father had brought him here once, but had warned him never to return alone. What did that matter now? Papa was gone: no one was left to care where Dilah went. He walked to the edge of the precipice and looked out over the white canyon. There was no sign of life. Far below, out of sight in the storm, the sea roared and crashed. The snow up here was thick and hard, and had been blown into strange shapes by the wind. Heartbroken, he walked along the clifftop, the wind whirling around him and snatching at his fur.

The clouds grew heavier, as if they'd been coated in dark-blue paint. His surroundings

became blurred. But then Dilah caught sight of something moving through the snow in front of him. He squinted and slowed down, keeping a watchful eye. A skulk of foxes emerged from the flurry. There must've been a dozen and they quickly surrounded him, cutting him off from every means of escape, the cliff at his back. A pale-blue fox headed the group. He looked like an ice sculpture: nearly translucent. He had thick fur, an air of arrogance, and a deep scar etched across his right eye.

'You must be Dilah,' the grim-faced fox said. His tone was chillier than the piercing wind.

'Who . . . who are you?' Dilah replied nervously, his voice muffled by the package still dangling from his mouth.

'My name is Jens, patriarch of the Arctic foxes,' the blue fox rasped, stepping forward. 'That parcel must be the moonstone. Carl, my old friend, it seems that you're correct,' he said, a faint smile spreading across his face.

Moonstone? Was that what was in the parcel? How could a stone guide him to Ulla's treasure?

'I told you I was there when Grey gave that

old thing to Blizzard,' a sly voice replied. A lean white fox emerged from behind Jens. *He must be Carl*, thought Dilah, confused and scared in equal measure. Carl's limbs were long and slender, his eyes yellow, deep-set and bloodshot. Dilah shivered. One of Carl's hind legs was dragging, as though he'd been seriously injured.

'What do you want?' Dilah asked.

Jens slowly approached Dilah, never taking his eyes off him, speaking in a low voice. 'Child, you're so young – and all alone out here in the wilderness. You have no use for the moonstone, but we need it. Come now – hand it over. In return, I can offer you safety, food and warmth.'

Dilah held the little package tightly between his teeth as he surveyed the pack of blue foxes, snow swirling around them. Their eyes were hard and cold; he couldn't imagine finding safety with them, despite Jens's coaxing words. Besides, his mother had entrusted this parcel – this moonstone, as Jens had called it – to him before she died. No matter what, he wasn't handing it over to anyone else. He suddenly felt braver. A low growl hummed in his throat. He was ready to fight to the death. 'No,' he said. 'You'd better give up and leave me alone.'

'Come now, child, don't be this way. You're frightened – but there's nothing to fear,' Jens said, speaking slowly. 'As the patriarch of the foxes, I can promise you that as long as you give us the moonstone, no one will harm you.' He and the other foxes drew closer to Dilah, tightening the circle around him.

Dilah backed up towards the edge of the cliff, determined not to surrender the moonstone. *At least if I die*, he thought, *I'll be with Mama and Papa again.*

'Let's just take it, Jens,' Carl snapped, his red-rimmed eyes staring savagely at Dilah.

'My mama left me this parcel. I'll never let you have it!' Dilah said, backing up towards the cliff edge.

Anger flickered across Jens's face. The blue fox roared, his rage so sudden and so powerful that it took Dilah's breath away. At the same time, the vicious half-circle of foxes tightened further. 'You'll die if you fall,' Jens said, anger simmering under his calm voice. 'I don't believe you'll jump. So before I let Carl have his way –' the white fox growled in appreciation – 'I'm giving you one last chance. Hand over the stone, or Carl and the rest of my pack will rip you to shreds.' There was a malicious glint in the foxes' eyes as they bared their teeth and claws, closing in on Dilah.

Dilah edged back further and nearly lost his footing. Clumps of snow fell into the chasm at his feet. He glanced over his shoulder and was overcome with dizziness: it was a bottomless pit.

In a split second, a white shape lunged at him with astonishing speed. Dilah didn't have time to think: he clamped down on the leather parcel, squeezed his eyes shut, and leapt off the cliff. Carl's teeth closed down on a tuft of his neck fur, but it was too late: Dilah fell away from the fox's grip, plummeting into the abyss alongside the snowflakes. The foxes' surprised cries gradually disappeared, the cold wind piercing Dilah's fur.

CHAPTER 2

The Moonstone

ittle by little, Dilah became aware of the hard ground, cool sea breeze, and salty air. He slowly opened his eyes, the glare of the sun beating on his face, the whoosh of waves crashing in his ears. *I am still alive.*

The blue fox. The white blur of shadow, the snap of sharp teeth and the stomach-turning fall – it felt like a long, confusing dream.

The snowstorm had stopped, the sky now clear and bright. Giant floating icebergs sparkled in the sun, and the surf gleefully pounded the rocks that lined the shore. A gust of wind splashed the ice-cold spray in Dilah's direction. He lay on a large, flat rock. How long had he been out of it?

'Mate, you're finally awake!' A small round head popped into Dilah's view. Dilah sprang to his feet in surprise and bumped smack into it.

Dilah instantly saw stars and felt as if everything was spinning. 'Ow!' cried the head. Dilah steadied himself and stood up – more slowly, this time. The owner of the head was a strange

fellow: short and squat, with huge, watery eyes and a velvety body. He was the spitting image of a glutinous rice ball.

A seal!

The seal rubbed his head with a large flipper, cursing up a storm.

'Cripes! Did you do that on purpose?' the seal huffed, furrowing his bushy eyebrows. 'You scoundrel, last night I pulled you out of the sea. It just about killed me!'

'You – you saved me?' Dilah asked, rubbing his own throbbing head.

'Of course! How else do you think you got here? I nearly passed out dragging you to shore, and you thank me by banging me on the head!'

'I'm so sorry!' Dilah felt awful.

Suddenly, the seal started to wheeze, his big brown eyes crinkling up.

Dilah was puzzled. Was there something wrong with the seal? Had he knocked the sense right out of him? He felt guilty. 'Are you OK?'

The seal wheezed harder, a tear trickling from his eye. Dilah realized he was laughing. 'It's so easy to fool you,' the seal chuckled at last, covering his mouth with a flipper. 'And a lot of fun!'

'Fun? You made me feel terrible!' Dilah said, torn between annoyance and relief. 'But I'm glad you're all right. How did you find me?'

'I was in the area searching for cod when something fell from the sky,' the seal said, waving his flippers. 'Then *plop* – the water splashed *this* high!' He raised a flipper up as high as he could reach. 'Then I grabbed you by the neck and dragged you to shore.'

Dilah shook the remaining beads of water off his body, his fur fluffing up wildly, and took in his surroundings. Far above, a towering cliff was covered with thick snow and ice. That's where he'd jumped from. He'd been lucky: the wind must've blown him out into the water as he fell.

'Anyway, my name's Egbert – but you can call me Egg. My mum called me a "bad egg" when I was a pup, and I guess it stuck.' The seal clapped his flippers together. 'And you?'

'I'm Dilah,' he said, a smile tugging at his lips. He couldn't help but warm to Egg.

'Dilah, there was a huge snowstorm last night. How'd you end up falling into the sea? If I'd found you any later, you might've . . .' Egg pretended to choke his own neck with his flippers and played dead.

Dilah laughed. 'I was . . .' But his mind went blank – the dreamlike memory had slipped away. Then, two words flashed through his mind: *the moonstone.* Dilah looked around in alarm – where was the parcel?

'My parcel!' He panicked. He must've dropped it when he'd fallen into the sea – the one thing he had from his mother! 'Have you seen my parcel?' he asked Egg.

'Parcel?' Egg frowned. 'I haven't . . .'

'Argh!' Dilah's blood froze and he sunk to his haunches. If he'd lost the moonstone, how would he ever find the secret treasure? How would he honour his parents' memory?

'Do you mean this?' Egg smirked, dangling a leather parcel in front of Dilah.

'That *really* wasn't funny!' Dilah cried out, his blood instantly thawing as he grabbed the leather package from Egg's flipper.

'What is it? Must be pretty special to have you so worked up,' Egg said, leaning forward curiously.

'It's called a moonstone, I think,' Dilah said, unwrapping the parcel. 'But I haven't actually seen it yet . . . let's take a look!'

The moment the parcel was opened, the two little animals' eyes widened. It was indeed a stone, but unlike any either had ever seen before. It gleamed with a beautiful blue light. Egg gasped.

'It's like the aurora, isn't it?' breathed Dilah, picturing the twisting blue-green beams that shimmered in the Arctic night sky. As he watched, the light danced and flickered like a flame, blazing in spite of the bright sunlight. Dilah noticed a small, golden crescent moon carved into the centre of the stone.

'Wow – it's beautiful!' he said in wonder.

'Sure is,' said Egg. 'Hey, what's this?' He pointed to a line of text on the untied leather.

Dilah gingerly nudged the moonstone off to the side and plucked at the piece of leather, carefully examining it in the sun. A line of gilded script was inscribed on its front:

I am not a worldly object;
I do not belong in this world.

On the reverse side, there was a picture of two foxes. They sat back to back, looking both charming and bashful with their exquisite curled-up tails, enchanting eyes, and long lashes. Between the arch of their tails, there was a poem, which Dilah read aloud:

I was formed in the Arctic.
I bring hope and guide the way.
I'm filled with sky and moon, on behalf
of the northern night.
More than a thousand years before,
I was unearthed one fateful eve.
As soon as I was touched by Ulla's hand,
I took charge of the wheel of life and death.
From then on, desire was born . . .
I shall follow my new master,
in search of my other half.

The sound of the waves faded away as Dilah read. It was as if everything around them had stopped, plunging them into silence.

'It's not really a poem, is it?' Egg asked, shaking his head. 'It's a riddle. Do you understand it? I don't think I do!'

Dilah remembered what his mother had told him: *Legend has it that the patron saint of the Arctic foxes, Ulla, created a secret treasure like no other. It contains an incredible magic that can turn animals into humans . . . There's something hidden beneath the dirt in the deepest part of our den that can lead you to Ulla's secret treasure . . .*

This riddle mentioned Ulla too, and said it would 'guide the way' – like his mama had promised. But what was this 'other half' – was that the treasure? And there wasn't anything in there about turning into a human. 'No,' said Dilah, frowning. 'I don't understand it either.'

Dilah noticed a faint line of text below the picture of the two foxes. He studied it closely, sticking his face up to the leather – it was a complex script written in strange, picture-like symbols.

'What's that?' Egg asked.

'I'm not sure. I don't recognize the language

at all. Perhaps it was written a long time ago,' Dilah said. What did these strange symbols mean? Did they have something to do with the origins of the moonstone? Or perhaps with how to use it?

'Wait . . .' Egg said, his eyes growing distant and thoughtful.

'What is it?' Dilah asked.

'I've seen similar symbols before . . . Let me think, where was that . . . ?' Egg wrinkled his eyebrows, clearly trying hard to remember. He shuffled over to the shore, gazing at the seemingly bottomless sea, tilting his head and lightly tapping it with one flipper.

'Ah!' Egg spun around and shouted excitedly. 'Grandpa Turtle! I remember, I saw these symbols on his shell!'

'Grandpa Turtle?' Dilah repeated. He tried to remember what his mama had told him of turtles. 'Is that a kind of fish with a stone on its back?'

'*With a stone on its back?*' Egg doubled over with laughter. 'Not exactly! You'll see. I think we should go and talk to him.'

Dilah felt a spark of hope. 'So he can understand these kinds of symbols?'

'Of course. He's no ordinary sea turtle! He's in the Arctic for a start! But he hasn't always been – he's more than two hundred years old, a world traveller who's seen it all. He knows loads of languages and even understands a bit about human civilizations. The story goes that he even knows why ships can swim! If ever there's something I don't understand, like the behaviour of white dolphins, or how to find flying fish in the North Sea, or where whales swim off to during winter, I'll go ask him.'

'Wow!' Dilah said, trying to imagine what a two-hundred-year-old sea turtle might look like. 'He sounds really impressive.'

'He is . . . but he can be a bit devious, and he has a unique hobby – he likes to collect treasures from all over the world and trade them with other animals. He's seen so many treasures. He might've heard something about the moonstone.' Egg had a glint in his eyes.

'Wonderful!' Dilah said, delighted. 'But do you know where he is?'

'I saw him recently. He swims slowly and loves to bask in the sun, so he can't be too far from where I passed him. If we head west along the coast, I'm sure we'll bump into him.'

'Then let's go!' Dilah said, jumping to his feet and chasing his tail in excitement.

Before they set off, Egg dove into the sea, retrieved a bundle of thin seaweed from the bottom, and wrapped it around the leather parcel. He hung the parcel carefully from Dilah's neck. Then he led him west, swimming close to the shoreline while Dilah padded along the beach on foot.

As evening approached, the western sky burnt bright scarlet, the glow of the setting sun illuminating the sandy beach, Dilah's shadow growing longer and longer. Dilah was about to step on to a fiery red rock when he realized it was moving, and quickly withdrew his paw, darting backwards. He lowered himself on to his haunches, his fur bristling, and eyed the moving rock curiously as two sharp pincers emerged from under the huge dome of its upper half. It was a crab, Dilah realized, his eyes widening.

'Hey, watch where you're stepping!' the crab scolded him, brandishing his gigantic pincers and inching closer to the sea. 'You inlanders: you've got no manners.'

'Fred?' Egg had swum up on to the beach, noticing Dilah had stopped.

'Hey, Egg, old pal!' As soon as he saw Egg, the crab's anger melted away, and he smiled.

'Fancy meeting you here,' said Egg. 'Didn't you say you were going on holiday to Hawaii?'

'Well, well, as you know, I say a lot of things, but I don't always mean all of them . . .' Fred said, looking away in embarrassment.

'Have you seen Grandpa Turtle around here?' Egg asked.

'Grandpa Turtle? As you know, I'm quite the social butterfly, so I'm not sure which one you're talking about.' Fred's beady eyes fixed on Dilah, measuring him up.

'*The* Grandpa Turtle! The one you frequently do business with – you know. *Grandpa Turtle*.' Egg flapped his flippers in exasperation.

'Oh, *that* one! As soon as you said the name, I thought you might mean him, that sly old crook!'

'What? I thought you two were friends?' Egg asked, wriggling his eyebrows.

'We used to be, but not any more!' Fred grumbled angrily. 'A few days ago, I gave him a black pearl found in the Norwegian strait in exchange for two tuna – I'd planned on saving them for winter. But he carved up a swordfish's mouth and passed it off to me as tuna. Swordfish indeed! The taste just can't compare!'

But then the crab shrugged, raising his two pincers and spreading his claws. 'Then again, I didn't suffer a loss, either: I actually gave him a white pearl that I'd dyed black with squid ink. That stupid turtle is too old to see clearly – he couldn't tell it was fake!' His tiny eyes narrowed with laughter, and he lightly clapped his pincers together.

'You say that Grandpa Turtle's a crook, but aren't you one as well?' Egg asked, raising an eyebrow.

Dilah smiled. It sounded like the two old

crooks were as bad as each other!

'I – I—' Fred stuck his head in the sand and said no more.

Egg and Dilah glanced at each other. 'Anyway . . . do you know where Grandpa Turtle is?' Egg asked the lump of sand where Fred had buried his head, speaking a little louder to compensate. 'We're looking for him.'

'Of course,' Fred replied, his voice muffled – he pulled out his head and squinted up at Egg. 'You're heading in the wrong direction. He's collecting pearls and jewels on the eastern shore!'

'Eastern shore? Are you sure? That's strange . . .' Egg said. He wasn't buying it.

'Why would I trick you? We made our trade on the eastern shore. If you turn back now, you can still catch him!' Fred urged.

'Is that so?' Egg said. He reached out suddenly with his flipper and pinned Fred down in the sand. 'You're lying!' he said.

'Hey, hey, Egg! What're you trying to do?' Fred cried out in panic. Egg pushed him deeper into the sand. Fred frantically flailed his claws, struggling to get up.

'Tell me the truth, Fred,' Egg said. 'I know you, and I know you're going to tell me, so spit it out!'

Sure enough, after wearing himself out struggling to no avail, Fred finally slumped into the sand and raised a single claw in surrender. Dilah couldn't help giggling.

'All right, all right, mate,' said the crab, 'I was just joking around with you and your friend – easy, easy! Grandpa Turtle is just up ahead looking for rare pink pearls.' Fred's small, shiny black eyes pleaded with Egg. 'Now, let me go!'

Egg slowly withdrew his flipper, grinning in satisfaction.

Fred scurried toward the sea, turning back to holler, 'You blasted seal! I won't let you get away with this again!' With that, he dove into the water, leaving behind a small trail of snow-white foam floating on the surface. Dilah and Egg looked at each other.

'Every. Single. Time,' Egg said, grinning.

They continued along the coastline. The

winter sun was low in the sky now, but it was holding itself above the horizon for a little longer with each passing day. Spring was on its way: the air was warming up, the icebergs were melting, and flocks of seabirds filled the air.

At last, a huge, green rock loomed out against the golden sand.

'That's him!' Egg said, under his breath.

'Really?' Dilah cocked his head. He couldn't see it! The rock was a crude half-sphere, glowing bright green in the sun as if covered with seaweed or moss. But as they drew closer, he started to pick out distinctly un-rocklike details. For instance, the bottom of the rock was scalloped like the hemline of a skirt, and there were peculiar zigzags and criss-crosses etched on the surface, like the paths and passageways of a labyrinth. What's more, a circle of strange lace-like symbols traced the lower part of the rock. Egg had been right: they really did resemble the symbols on the moonstone's leather parcel!

'Grandpa Turtle!' Egg called.

'Hmm . . . hello?' an old hoarse voice

grumbled from the rock. At the same time, a head, four flippers, and a tail slowly poked out.

The turtle's skin was pale green and heavily wrinkled, his face a web of creases. His eyelids drooped halfway down and there were heavy bags beneath his bulging eyes. His cheeks sagged like curtains as he raised his head and stared listlessly down his beak at the two uninvited guests.

'Grandpa Turtle, it's me, Egg!'

'Egg? I haven't heard of you . . .' He squinted. 'Are you a walrus?' He reached into his shell and pulled out a pair of delicate gold-rimmed glasses. He put on the glasses and scrutinized Egg with small, wrinkle-set eyes.

Egg had just started explaining who he was when Grandpa Turtle interrupted him. 'Ah, yes, you're that seal pup who's always asking me strange questions . . . I'm sorry, I'm not as young as I used to be – my eyesight's going, my memory's going, my mind wanders . . .' he said, drawing out each word. 'I saw your parents not that long ago . . .'

'Oh? How are they?' Egg asked with concern.

'They've seen better days. They asked after you,' the old turtle said. Then he frowned. 'Hey, how'd you know I was here, anyway?'

'I ran into Fred on the way. He said you were here searching for rare—'

'Pink pearls? Hmph! That rascal told me he'd found some on the ocean floor nearby. I've been searching and searching, and nothing! Zip! Zilch! Nada!' His spectacles were all steamed up. 'He also tricked me into giving him two swordfish for a white pearl. I promise you, one day he's going to end up on a human's dinner table!'

At the thought of Grandpa Turtle and Fred cheating each other, and each complaining about being cheated by the other, Dilah sniggered.

'Hmm . . . and who might you be?' The turtle's glasses had cleared up. They magnified his round eyes as he peered down at Dilah.

'Grandpa Turtle,' said Egg, 'this is my friend, Dilah. We'd like to ask you some questions.'

'Oh? Ask me some questions? But I'm just an old turtle. My eyesight's going, my memory's going, my mind wanders. I don't know anything . . .' Grandpa Turtle looked at Egg expectantly.

'Pah! There's nothing in this world that Grandpa Turtle doesn't know!' Egg smiled winningly. *He's certainly quick to lay on the sweet talk*, thought Dilah.

'Everyone calls me a walking encyclopedia!' the turtle chuckled, his loose wrinkly throat wobbling. 'But I never share my knowledge for free . . .' He gave Egg a sidelong glance.

'Oh, of course,' Egg said. 'What would you like?'

'Five tunas.' *Suddenly the old turtle doesn't sound so doddery!*

'That's outrageous. I'll catch you three,' Egg immediately countered.

The old sea turtle shook his wrinkled head in disappointment. 'I'm just an old turtle. My eyesight's going, my memory's going, my mind wanders. I can't afford to hand out my precious knowledge for a measly three tuna.'

'In this season, it's hard to find tuna,' Egg pleaded.

'Oh, look at me, an old bag of bones!' Grandpa Turtle sighed. 'All right, for your poor mother's sake, how about four?' He proposed, narrowing his eyes.

Egg nodded.

'It's a deal!' Grandpa Turtle boomed at the top of his lungs, instantly perking up. 'So . . . what would you and this little fox like to ask me?' He watched Dilah with great interest, his neck outstretched, his voice low and gravelly.

Dilah glanced at Egg doubtfully. The seal nodded and Dilah took a deep breath. 'I'd like you to help me figure out what these symbols mean.' He removed the parcel from his neck and opened it. In an instant, it was as if a blue fire had been lit upon the white sand, as the moonstone glittered in the last rays of the sun.

'Good heavens!' Grandpa Turtle gasped, his mouth agape. 'That . . . that's . . .' He stared in shock at the moonstone, its curved surface reflecting its own light.

'They call it the moonstone,' Dilah said.

'Moonstone? I've never seen such a gorgeous treasure . . . How many untold treasures are you

Arctic foxes hiding?' the old sea turtle muttered, greedily eyeing the moonstone. 'Anyway, you mentioned something about symbols . . .'

Dilah picked up the leather and held it close to Grandpa Turtle's eyes.

'Hmm, let me have a look . . . *I was formed in the Arctic. I bring hope and guide the way . . . I shall follow my new master, in search of my other half . . .*' Grandpa Turtle took his time reciting the poem, before apparently absorbing each of the symbols below it one by one.

'There's a line below the riddle,' Dilah said. 'It's written in the same symbols that are on your shell. Can you read it?'

There was a moment of silence.

'Hmm . . . this is Classical Animalese.'

'Classical Animalese?' Dilah and Egg said in unison.

'Yes. It's an ancient animal script. Almost all of the animals who can read it are extinct,' he said, a little sadly. 'Lucky for you, I'm still here. If my understanding is correct, it means: "When you're lost, let the sky lead the way."'

the turtle slowly explained.

'When you're lost, let the sky lead the way . . .' Dilah repeated, frowning and gazing up at the darkening blue sky, as if it contained the answers.

'So then,' said the old turtle, 'it seems that the rumour is true – the patron saint of the white foxes really *did* leave behind a treasure for his descendants. I can make out a little of the poem, but it's hard to understand . . .' Grandpa Turtle was lost in thought, an inscrutable expression flitting across his face.

'What *can* you make out?' Dilah asked eagerly.

'Hmm . . . I'm afraid not, little fox. I've already answered your question.' The old turtle's eyelids fluttered slightly and closed.

'Well then, thank you,' Dilah said, slightly disappointed.

'I'll give you ten pieces of gold coral and fifty black pearls in exchange for the moonstone,' the turtle offered, motioning towards the stone with his front flipper, extending a single claw towards it . . .

Dilah snatched the stone out of reach. 'No way. My mama gave this to me. It's priceless.'

'Hmph, stubborn little fellow. I'm warning you, this stone will bring you danger—'

'I'm not afraid!'

'Ha! More fool you. Well then, make good use of this stone; it will change your fate,' Grandpa Turtle said, gazing at Dilah with surprisingly kind eyes. 'I've spent long enough in the sun, and I've rested enough, and so I think it's time for me to set out on another treasure hunt.' He tucked his glasses into his shell and trudged toward the sea. 'You can wait to give me those four tuna until you've had a chance to catch them, little seal, but beware: I'll add interest . . . Also, Egg, if you have time, go see your parents. After all, they're getting on in years.'

'I know. Thank you, Grandpa Turtle!' Egg said with a smile.

The huge old turtle crawled to the shore, cast a mysterious grin back at Dilah, the expression on his face unreadable, then slowly sank into the sea, vanishing into the vast waters.

'Dilah, what does the moonstone have to do with your patron saint?' Egg asked.

Dilah sat down, wrapping his large fluffy tail carefully around his paws. It was time to tell Egg everything – after all, he had proved himself a true friend. 'Before she died, Mama told me that the moonstone could lead me to a great, secret treasure left by Ulla.'

'What's the secret treasure?'

'I'm not sure. I guess it wouldn't be a secret if everyone knew . . . but supposedly, it can turn animals into humans.'

'Turn animals into humans?!' Egg's eyes grew large with excitement. But then he frowned. 'So you plan to find the treasure and then turn into a human?'

Dilah remembered the human family he used to watch, how varied and exciting and full of possibility their lives had appeared to be, and he nodded. 'Yes, that's my dream!'

'Wow!' Egg said admiringly . . . and maybe a little sceptically. 'Based on what Grandpa Turtle said, have you figured out how the moonstone works?'

'"When you're lost, let the sky lead the way" . . . Nope, I still have no idea,' Dilah sighed.

'Maybe try opening the parcel beneath the sky?' Egg suggested.

'Just now it was open beneath the sky, and nothing happened,' Dilah pointed out.

After a thoughtful pause, Egg spoke again. 'Maybe we're misinterpreting it? Like, maybe you're supposed to throw it in the air, or place it under a particular part of the sky?'

Dilah shrugged. 'Let's try.' He tossed the moonstone in the air. It arched high, spinning as it fell. It bumped on to Egg's head, then rolled to the ground. Nothing special happened.

'Dilah, over here – try it over here!' The two friends tried over and over as the sun slunk into the sea, leaving a red halo on the horizon.

As night fell, they decided to rest. Stars dotted the sky, gazing down with twinkling, blinking eyes. The full moon rose, spilling bright light on to the earth. The sea was pitch-dark beneath the moonlight, rising and falling, wave after wave crashing onto the shore. One would wash over Dilah's and Egg's feet, then another, dissolving into snow-white foam with a splash. Scowling, Dilah sat on the beach, frustrated that they hadn't figured out how to use the moonstone, even after consulting Grandpa Turtle. He felt guilty too – Egg had committed to paying four fish for the old turtle's useless translation.

'Look, the moon tonight is so pretty!' said Egg, craning his neck.

'The moon!' *Eureka!* Dilah scrambled to his feet and gazed up at the mysterious moon.

Memories whirled in Dilah's mind. *I'm filled with sky and moon . . . when you're lost, let the sky lead the way . . .* 'It's the *moon*stone!' he cried.

'What? So what?' Egg looked confused.

'That's how the moonstone works!' Dilah said, jumping up and down excitedly. 'Moon-light!'

He scrambled to unwrap the leather parcel, exposing the stone to the moonlight. They held their breath, eyes fixed on the moonstone. At first, nothing happened – but then, the small crescent moon in the centre of the moonstone began glowing with a golden light.

'Look!' squeaked Egg excitedly.

Slowly, the moon symbol started to turn. It turned faster and faster until it was a spinning, blurry circle inside the blue crystal of the stone. And then it started to slow down, slower and slower, eventually drawing to a stop. The two ends of the crescent were pointing south-east, like a pair of arrows. A line of light beamed out from the stone, lighting the path ahead, gently pulsing like a heartbeat.

'We did it! Ulla's treasure is that way!' Dilah's eyes glistened.

Egg cheered, clapping his flippers. 'We did it! We did it!

Dilah kept his eyes on the magical stone, his heart beating in time to its golden light. He'd risked his life for this stone and now, at last, he'd come to understand its secret. As the sea breeze gently ruffled his snow-white fur, he gazed south-east.

'Egg, I'm one step closer to my dream,' Dilah said. 'Thank you, my friend. I couldn't have done it without your help. I'll leave first thing tomorrow.'

'What? So soon!'

'Yes. I just hope the blue foxes think I'm dead, and that the moonstone is lost for ever in the sea, but if they catch my trail . . .' He shook his head. 'My best chance is a long head start.'

'All right, all right.' Egg shook his fluffy little head in sadness. 'I should go home to my parents – it sounds like they're worried about me. It looks like it's time for us to say goodbye . . .'

Dilah and Egg faced each other and the mood was suddenly sombre. Now that he knew how to use the moonstone, Dilah should've been on top of the world . . . but how could he be happy at the thought of saying goodbye to Egg, the only friend he'd ever had? Part of him regretted that they'd figured out how to use the moonstone so quickly.

As the lonely waves washed over the rocks again and again, Dilah and Egg lay wordlessly on the beach, neither of them sleeping, neither of them talking. They simply lay down together and watched the stars. Perhaps this kind of silence was the only way they could think of to say goodbye.

Daylight broke to draw them from the night, the sharp, clear trills of seabirds ringing out in the distance. The sky was a sad sort of pale blue streaked with faint white light, like something you'd find on an artist's palette.

'You'd better hit the road, mate!' Egg said, a forced cheeriness in his voice. 'And I'd better hit the waves.'

'Egg, I won't forget you,' Dilah said, smiling. He lowered his head, suddenly bashful. 'You know, last night, you also saw which way the moonstone pointed, didn't you? In case . . . I mean . . . just in case you decide you'd also like to become human, you can find me by heading in that direction.' Even if there was only a glimmer of hope, he wanted to see Egg again.

Egg looked genuinely moved, his whiskers quivering. 'OK, Dilah, I'll follow you someday. We'll meet again! Let's swear on it!' Egg extended a large flipper.

Dilah's furry paw reached out to touch the flipper for a moment, before Egg pulled it back and slapped it against Dilah's raised paw in a high five.

The young seal slid into the sea until the water was just below his neck. He flipped over, his tail skimming the surface, creating a glittering spray.

'Be careful out there!' Dilah called out, following Egg with his eyes as he disappeared under the surface.

'You too!' Egg's small head poked out of the water. He waved at Dilah, then turned and vanished into the blue.

Dilah quietly watched Egg disappear, his heart rising and falling like the surf. Since childhood, Dilah had followed his parents and stayed away from other foxes. He'd never had even one friend – until he'd met Egg, he hadn't truly realized what friendship was. He hoped Egg would always be happy, whether or not he kept his promise and followed Dilah in the end. At least the little seal had his parents: he should appreciate them while he could. Dilah felt a pang in his heart at the thought of his own family.

He turned away from the sea and headed south-east, leaving clover-shaped prints on the sand – from now on, whatever difficulties came his way, he'd have to face them alone.

CHAPTER 3

The Forest Watchman

Dilah ran farther and farther away from the sea, the bright blue waves giving way to a plain covered in snow and ice. Rocks lay bare in the bitter wind. In the distance, snow-capped mountains towered up to the clouds. He shot across the barren land, the moonstone swaying to and fro around his neck. He ran for days, hardly stopping to rest or eat what little food he found – a half-frozen lemming sustained him for part of the journey, but his stomach was soon painful with constant hunger. Eventually, he spotted a line of pine trees at the end of the snowfield. These were the first plants he'd seen for ages. Filled with hope, he bounded towards them.

Dilah stood at the edge of the forest and sniffed, the cold wind slowly pushing him on. He ran. One tree, two trees, three trees . . . soon the slender trunks were whizzing by as Dilah bounded over softer earth, the sharp pine smell filling his nose as he crushed their needles under his paws. The old, soldier-like trees soared proudly into the clouds, their branches

cloaked in thick snow. Dilah kicked playfully at the empty pinecones strewn around, his hunger temporarily forgotten.

In time, though, the cold and hunger wore away his resolve. His head was heavy, his stomach was growling, and his paws felt like they'd been weighed down with lead. Although squirrels and birds flitted in the trees, Dilah wasn't sure he was fast or strong enough to catch one.

It wasn't long before darkness fell again; soon, it was as though a black velvet curtain had been drawn across the sky. The stars and moon only shed the faintest of light, as if they too were exhausted. Dilah passed a tall, perfectly straight pine tree, noticing something unusual hanging from a broken branch. Was that a top hat? He frowned, then shivered with a mixture of fear and excitement. Humans must be near.

The more he walked along in the dark, the more he began to lose hope of ever finding food and shelter. But after a while, he saw a yellow light up ahead. He crept towards it. What could it be?

The light grew larger and took on a square shape. It was coming from an old stone cottage that stood alone in the forest, surrounded by silver trees. The walls were made of grey stone, and the roof was blanketed in thick snow. A thin curl of smoke rose from the chimney. A small shovelled path led from the cottage's wooden door into the depths of the forest.

A single window was shedding the warm yellow light Dilah had seen from the trees. Through the frost on the glass, Dilah could make out a table set with several dishes. A pretty woman stood next to the table, holding a baby. She had a narrow face, deep-blue eyes and dark hair and wore a large striped jumper with a huge hole in one of the arms. A blond man with a slight build sat on one side, gobbling up the food on his plate. His hair was messy. Dilah thought he looked dishevelled but kind. As he shovelled food into his mouth, he pulled faces at the baby in the woman's arms. The woman smiled at the child then turned to the man, whispering something.

They look like a happy family, Dilah thought.

He warily approached the house, wondering whether he might be able to steal some food scraps from the outside bins.

Just then, the wooden door to the cottage creaked open, a beam of light unfurling like a shining carpet throughout the never-ending darkness of the forest. The man stepped out, wearing a faded wool coat. The light from the door elongated his shadow. He picked up a pail from beside the door and was just about to head back inside when his eyes fell on Dilah. Instinctively, Dilah took a few steps back.

'You'll never believe this, Lily, come quick!' the man called toward the house in surprise, blowing white puffs of breath.

'What? Oh, Mideo!' Lily came outside with the baby in her arms, gasping when she saw Dilah. 'It's so beautiful!' Her eyes were as round as saucers.

'It's rare to see an Arctic fox around these parts. This little fellow must be lost.'

'Wait – what's that around its neck?' Lily asked, spotting Dilah's leather parcel.

'Hmm. Someone must have put it there!'

'Could it be an abandoned pet from town?' Lily asked.

'I've never heard of anyone in town keeping an Arctic fox,' Mideo said, perplexed. 'In fact, I've never heard of *anyone* keeping an Arctic fox!'

'It's strange,' Lily said, walking slowly towards Dilah, eager to get a better look at the package that hung from his neck.

Dilah took a few large steps back, his eyes fixed on the woman's every move. He knew they didn't mean any harm, but he wasn't going to let them touch the moonstone.

'It seems like it doesn't want us to get too close. We have to help it, though – it's freezing out here,' Lily said, turning around and going inside.

'Shall we give it the leftover chicken from tonight? It looks like it's starving,' Mideo said.

In a few minutes, Lily and Mideo returned without the baby, carrying a plate stacked with meat and bones.

Lily set the plate carefully on to the snow beneath the window. Dilah eyed the food, the delicious smell wafting into his nostrils as the cold wind blew. He was salivating. He glanced up at the couple, waiting for them to go back inside. He didn't trust them – not yet.

'Let's go. It looks scared,' Mideo said, turning to Lily then heading back into the house and gently closing the door behind them.

Dilah threw himself at the meat and wolfed it down so quickly that he barely even tasted it. He hardly noticed the two sets of eyes staring at him from the window above.

He chewed the meat from the last bone and burped in satisfaction. He was warmer now, and he could already feel his legs flooding with strength. He licked his snout and looked around. At some point, the light in the window had gone out, leaving behind only the silvery darkness and stillness. Dilah circled the stone cottage, feeling emboldened. He came upon a small road, the snow imprinted with layers of tyre tread marks. *This probably leads to a town*, he thought, *or wherever the humans go for supplies*. Behind the stone cottage, there was a thatched shed, its roof covered with thick snow. Dilah followed Mideo and Lily's footprints through the open door. There was no wind inside, so it was noticeably warmer. In the darkness, Dilah made out stacks of wood that the couple probably used for cooking and heating the fireplace. There was an old motorbike too, and a broken wooden cabinet.

He stretched a bit, then found a comfortable pile of straw and lay down, curling into a ball, shielding his eyes with his big bushy tail.

The next morning, Dilah opened his eyes and stared in a daze at his surroundings, lit up in the soft grey light of dawn. Hearing the crunch of footsteps on the snow outside, he poked his head out of the shed and looked around. Mideo had just come back from the forest, wearing a thick cotton cap and the same faded coat from the night before. You could see the white fog of his breath, and his whole face was red from the cold. For reasons even Dilah himself didn't understand, a sense of kinship lured him out of the shed.

Mideo stopped and smiled at him. 'Aha –

when I saw your little paw prints this morning, I knew you hadn't left. You must've hidden in the shed, yes?' He chuckled. 'It's not a good idea for you to stay here – you need to go home as soon as you can!'

Dilah leant slightly forwards, peering kindly at Mideo. *Why isn't it good to stay here?* he wanted to ask. He thought it as loudly as he could, but Mideo clearly couldn't read his mind.

'Where on earth did you come from?' the man wondered aloud, gazing sympathetically at Dilah. 'Are you hungry? Don't worry – Lily's whipping up breakfast! I'm sure we can find some more leftovers for you.'

Mideo strode into the cottage. The kitchen light was on, and Dilah walked over to the window and peeked inside. Lily was busy slicing bread at the table, while Mideo stood beside her, trying to soothe the crying baby in his arms. Through the glass, Dilah could just about make out the sounds inside.

'Is the little fox still here?' Lily asked as she sliced.

'Yup. It spent the night in the shed. It seems to like it here.' Mideo looked at the baby he was holding.

'Put that old blanket down on the floor of the shed – it'll be warmer than straw on its own.' Lily placed the sliced bread on a plate and turned around, reaching for the jam in the cupboard. 'Ah! Can you get Leo to quiet down? My head's about to explode.' She frowned. Now the baby was crying even harder. Maybe Mideo was holding him wrong.

'Surely you're not thinking of keeping the fox as a pet?' Mideo joked. 'We shouldn't keep it here, really. It's a wild animal.'

'It's freezing out there. We can't just ignore it, we have to help it,' said Lily, and Dilah felt a warm glow of gratitude spread all through his body. 'Maybe when spring comes it'll go on its own. Besides, what about that parcel round its neck? Wild animals don't tend to have collars.'

Mideo nodded thoughtfully as he rocked the crying baby. 'Could it be something left by the original owner? An address? What do you think, Baby Leo?' Mideo scrunched up his face comically. The baby stopped crying and studied him curiously.

'It's rather strange,' Lily said. 'Anyway, you go ahead and eat. I'll feed the baby.' She took little Leo. Mideo sat at the table and started eating.

'If only it were a jewel hanging around its neck,' he said between bites. 'We could use a little cash injection.' Dilah's ears pricked up and he backed away slightly.

Lily snorted. 'I've never had any expectations of becoming rich!' She fed Leo his bottle, watching tenderly as his little face relaxed. When Lily spoke again, her voice was softer. 'But if only you would let those bigwig timber merchants cut down a few pine trees, things could be a little easier . . .'

'Lily, you know that's impossible,' Mideo said gently, his face serious. 'This is a national pine forest. It's my duty to protect it!'

Lily smiled. 'I married you because you're a good, honest man. I suppose if you allowed the trees to be cut down, then you wouldn't be you.

Besides, you and Leo are more than enough for me. What else could I ask for?'

The sun rose from behind the forest, cloaking the silver trees in glittering gold. Birds chirped up a storm and smoke puffed from the cottage chimney. Dilah paced for a bit, then went back to lie down in the shed. He didn't feel strong enough to continue on his journey, not just yet. Besides, hadn't Mideo said something about leftovers?

Sure enough, Mideo came out bundled up in his coat, one hand holding a plate, the other carrying a worn-out green blanket. He approached Dilah, who hurried nervously to the back of the shed, and spread the blanket out over the straw where Dilah had just been lying, gesturing that it was meant for him. Then he put the plate on the floor.

Dilah waited until Mideo had left, sniffed the food and dug in. The taste was different . . . sort of sweet, nothing like the lemming meat Dilah had eaten with his parents, or the fish Egg had brought him on the beach. It wasn't nutty, either. It was unlike anything he'd ever eaten before, but he quickly decided he liked it! He scoffed it down, then sprawled out on the soft, comfortable blanket. A feeling of contentment washed over Dilah – for the first time since Mama had died, he felt like he was home.

In a matter of days, Dilah packed on quite a bit of weight! He was living the high life, eating the family's leftovers – brought to him by Mideo three times a day – and snoozing in the shed. Lily often dropped by with baby Leo in her arms. Dilah liked the baby, who cooed and squealed at him in excitement, clapping his chubby hands. Dilah put on a show, chasing his tail and clowning around in the snow until Leo and Lily were both in fits of giggles.

Late one night, the sky was covered with black clouds. Outside the shed, there was only the howling of the cold wind and a darkness so thick you could cut it with a knife. The cottage light was off, the family of three sleeping soundly in the pitch-dark. Countless tiny snowflakes drifted outside, whirling in the bitter wind. Dilah was also fast asleep – until, all of a sudden, he was startled awake by a loud noise. His eyes snapped open, and his ears perked up. He raised his head and listened.

It was the rumble of an engine. A glimmer of light swept over the shed door. He crept out. A huge black truck crawled past the house and down the road, heading for the pine forest. Dilah cautiously trailed behind. The truck stopped near a cluster of towering pine trees and the doors opened. Driver and passengers hopped down from the front and back seats, one after another, five people in all. The one from the front seat was short and plump, with a small nose and beady eyes, and a cruel, hard expression on his face. He wore a tall black mink-fur hat and a black jacket that flapped open in the breeze. He was the spitting image of a fat black bat, Dilah thought. He stood at the head of the group, shining a torch among the pine trees while the other four men followed him.

The cruel-faced man stopped, pointing to the tree that had the black top hat hanging from a broken branch. He stood on his tiptoes and plucked it down, shaking out the snow inside. 'This is the one,' he said to the others. 'I marked it last time I was here. The others around here are good too.'

'Are these trees really all that valuable, Klaus?' one of the other men asked. He had a tired, worn face, Dilah thought, and he didn't look happy to be there in the forest. 'I mean, is it worth sneaking around in the middle of the night just to steal a few trees?'

'What? Of course! This is an extremely rare kind of pine! The material is uniform through-out, the texture is hard, the pliability is excellent – it'll fetch a pretty penny on the black market!' Klaus patted the trunk. 'Even if we only sell one, we'll be set for life!' He twirled the top hat in one hand. Dilah narrowed his eyes at the bat-like man. He didn't like him, not one bit.

'But, sir . . .' the other man started, hesi-tantly, 'can't we keep things above board and come during the day instead? We could pay Mideo handsomely if the tree's worth that much.'

Klaus shook his head. 'I've made him several offers, but he won't budge. He'd rather watch this precious timber rot than allow me to buy it from him. Pity – but he leaves me no choice.' He threw down the top hat with a flourish. 'OK, enough with the chit-chat. Let's get moving!'

The men got to work. They took a chainsaw and rope out of the truck and tied the rope around the tree. The chainsaw stuttered to life, a horrible buzzing noise echoing through the forest. Dilah took several steps backwards, his ears flattened, his heart pattering. He crouched in the snow, too frightened to move. When the saw came into contact with the tree trunk, the buzz grew louder and shriller. Dilah thought it sounded like a scream. After a few minutes there was an ear-splitting boom. The tall, ancient pine crashed to the ground, the vibrations rattling the snow from nearby trees. At that moment, a light went on in the cottage.

'Hurry up, you good-for-nothings!' Klaus hissed.

The cottage door creaked open. Mideo

stepped out holding a torch, struggling with his coat.

'Who's there?' Mideo pointed the beam into the dark woods. Even from afar, Dilah could see the fear and anger on his ashen face. 'Stop!' He ran towards the men, his breath pluming into the air, the torch beam casting crazy shadows among the trees. Dilah shivered in the snow, afraid for Mideo but unsure of how to help. 'Klaus?' Mideo said in disbelief, as he reached the group. 'What do you think you're doing? Stop this at once!'

'Good evening, Mideo. We meet again.'

Mideo's eyes widened as he caught sight of the pine tree lying on the ground, his entire body trembling with rage.

Klaus's men kept sawing at a second tree, which was ready to fall any second.

'Hold on! Stop! Stop!' Mideo gasped, charging at them.

'We won't stop. It's too late for that,' Klaus said coldly. 'You should have taken my original offer . . . but I am still willing to offer you some payment, as long as you promise not to—'

'Stop!' Mideo wasn't listening; he was tugging at the man holding the chainsaw with all his might, but the burly man shrugged him off. The second pine tree crashed to the snowy ground. Mideo looked on in despair. 'No . . . stop . . .' he cried, but his voice was weakened with grief. Dilah watched as Mideo's face hardened from despair to determination. He turned around and ran back towards the cottage.

'He's going to call the police! Stop him!' Klaus ordered his men.

Bang!

Dilah flinched in his hiding place. He watched, uncomprehending, as Mideo dropped to the ground with a thud. First, he smelt blood. Then he saw the gun, white smoke curling from its muzzle, held outstretched in the hand of one of Klaus's men. Slowly, the man lowered the weapon. Mideo lay as motionless as the fallen pine trees.

Dilah sucked in a big gulp of cool air. He couldn't bring himself to believe what was happening, but Mideo's breathing was fading.

They'd killed him and Dilah had done nothing.

'No – no—' Lily had run out of the stone cottage when she heard the gunshot. Now, she flung herself at Mideo's fallen body and pulled at his coat. 'No . . .' She hadn't even glanced at the men gathered among the trees, at how Klaus had snatched the gun from his man's hand.

Dilah wanted to leap out and warn Lily, rescue her somehow. But before he had a chance, he heard two booming sounds. Lily slumped over, her hand clasping her husband's.

Everything was quiet. The snow continued to fall.

Suddenly, baby Leo's cries rang out from the cottage, louder and more heart-wrenching than ever.

Klaus shoved the gun back into the hands of the man who'd shot Mideo. 'This will save us a lot of trouble in the long run. Go inside the house and see if anyone else is there. And disconnect the phone!'

The man rushed into the cottage with his gun while the others loaded the trunks on to the lorry. Little Leo was howling inside. Dilah's heart was in his throat.

The man stepped outside a few moments later. 'There's just the baby inside. Unless you . . .'

'Hmm.' Klaus took a deep breath. Then, he shook his head. 'Let's just leave it.' He wiped the sweat from his forehead, wrapped his black jacket tightly around his body and turned back towards the truck, deliberately bypassing Mideo and Lily.

Dilah was now hiding near the truck. When he saw the men heading in his direction, he clumsily backed away, accidentally stepping on a branch. *Snap.*

'Who's there?' Klaus nervously called out.

One of the men shined his flashlight on Dilah, breathing a sigh of relief. 'It's just a fox.'

Terrified that they would shoot him too, Dilah spun around and dashed into the forest. But no one followed him.

The truck sped off with a roar, leaving swirling snowflakes in its wake. Dilah walked over to Mideo and Lily. Their eyes were closed and they looked peaceful. He felt his own eyes sting. These two kind people, who'd made him feel at home for the first time since Mama had died, were no longer part of this world. But they'd left behind a spark: Baby Leo.

Leo was bawling at the top of his lungs now. Dilah bowed his head and emerged from the dark woods, the pine trees creaking softly in the breeze. He walked up the steps of the cottage, hesitated, then entered the building for the first time. It was warm inside and smelt of Mideo and Lily, of food and fire. The light was still on. Dilah padded towards the sound of crying, in the bedroom off the kitchen. Leo's mother had wrapped him in swaddling clothes and placed him on the bed. His large eyes glistened with tears. His scrunched-up little face was flushed red. His arms and legs were twisted, trying to break free from the swaddling clothes.

Dilah hopped up on the bed and looked at the teary-eyed baby, feeling a pang in his heart. He had blue eyes, just like his mother. Leo saw the fluffy fox approaching and abruptly stopped crying. Instead, he giggled, breaking into a wide, cheerful smile.

Outside, the snow was coming down harder and harder, big flakes falling and melting against the bedroom window.

Grief and anger gnawed at Dilah. This stone cottage was cut off from the world – there was no way he could leave poor orphaned Leo all alone with no one to care for him. Gripping the ribbon on the swaddling clothes with his teeth, Dilah lifted the baby off the bed and bolted out of the cottage, filled with determination. There was just one road here: the road that led to town. The only thing that Dilah could do to return the family's kindness was to bring the baby there, where someone else could look after him.

Dilah took one last look back at the cosy little home, clutching the swaddling clothes between his teeth. Then he barrelled down the snowy road. Soon, the baby was lulled asleep by the motion, despite the cold. Along the way, there was nothing but heavy darkness and snow falling from the sky. Dilah kept replaying the scene he'd just witnessed over and over in his mind – how quickly Mideo and Lily's happy lives had been cut short by other humans. For the first time, he wondered if he really wanted to be a human at all. How could they be so heartless?

He didn't know how long he'd been running, but soon the darkness thinned to grey and Dilah could see little Leo's face, red from the cold. A few specks of light shone through the snow flurries. These specks grew larger and larger, houses cropping up here and there alongside the road. Some of the windows blazed with light, and smoke hung over the rooftops. Dilah felt a strong surge of hope and relief; his strength was waning, but with people around he knew Leo would be saved.

Dilah shuttled back and forth among the houses, looking all around, hoping to find someone. He couldn't just leave Leo out here in the cold.

A red door screeched open, streaming light out onto the snowbanks. A woman stepped outside, a scarf wrapped around her head, thick cotton slippers on her feet. She padded over to the firewood stacked beside the fence, bending down to pick up a few logs. *Here's my chance*, thought Dilah. After shaking the snow off the wood, the woman started turning around to head back inside. At that moment, Dilah deliberately passed by and stood across from her on the other side of the fence, gazing at her expectantly.

After few moment's hesitation, she cautiously approached Dilah and peered down at the bundle dangling from his mouth. When her eyes fell on Leo's chilled red face, her terrified scream pierced the grey morning light.

The wood in her arms clattered to the ground.

Dilah set Leo down and started to back away, readying himself to run. But he was reluctant to leave until the woman picked Leo up. He wanted to know for sure that the baby was safe.

The woman's cries roused the sleepy village. Dogs barked. Several windows suddenly lit up. Some people pressed their faces against the window panes, others stuck their heads out the doors. A few simply put on their coats and came out to see what was going on.

'The fox . . . it was holding a baby . . .' the woman appeared to be in shock. She didn't approach the baby or Dilah, who slunk back, willing her to pick up Leo, who was now wailing thinly.

The village was suddenly full of life. Draped in blankets and coats, they poured out of their homes.

'Isn't this Lily's child?' a young woman called out. She rushed forward and gathered Leo up in her arms. 'Poor little mite, he's freezing cold.' She wrapped him up in her scarf and gazed down at him tenderly, and finally Dilah knew he was safe. He started to run – but he was surrounded. He headed towards a gap in the small crowd. 'That fox stole a baby!' someone cried out. 'Stop it!'

A wooden club came out of nowhere and struck Dilah's hind leg as he tried to run past. The pain was unbearable. He stumbled forward.

'Out of the way!' an old man in a sheepskin

hat fumed, aiming a shotgun at Dilah. Dilah's heart clenched and he tried to scramble away, his leg throbbing.

'Wait!' came another voice from the crowd. 'It didn't harm the child. Let it go.'

Whoever it was, and whatever the old man decided, the voice provided enough of a distraction for Dilah to escape. He jumped down a small slope on the side of the road and sprinted off into the wilderness.

Once he was a safe distance away, Dilah slowed down and rested amid the heavy, blowing snow. His heart was pounding, and his hind leg ached. But Leo was safe. He hoped the kind lady would adopt him. Either way, Mideo's and Lily's bodies would soon be discovered, and perhaps then the villagers would see that Dilah had never meant Leo any harm. He breathed a huge sigh of relief and relaxed a little.

Once he'd caught his breath, Dilah raced off again, leaving another trail of clover-shaped paw prints in the snow.

CHAPTER 4

A Flash of Wisdom

After what felt like for ever, the snow eventually stopped – but this was small relief. Dilah limped along, the howling wind stabbing at him like a knife. He imagined Leo somewhere warm, sleeping safe and sound, and a flame blazed in Dilah's heart, chasing away the bitter cold. He continued south-east, the moonstone dangling from his neck.

Dilah had been travelling for days when he stepped on to a frozen river and hesitated, daunted by his desolate surroundings. Where was the moonstone leading him, and when would he arrive? All he could see was white. There was nothing here to satisfy his hunger. At a loss, he gazed into the distance and forced himself to trudge on. There seemed to be no end to this ice-covered earth. Hunger and despair gnawed at him. At last, he plopped down on a block of ice. How he missed the pine forest, the little stone cottage, poor Mideo and Lily, the baby and the shed, and all of the food the family had left for him. He missed Egg and their time together travelling along the coast. But most of all, he missed his mama and papa. Suddenly, it was difficult to hold on to his dream. He just wanted to sleep. Maybe then, he could forget everything he had lost.

The sky was clear and cloudless. As Dilah looked up, blinking away his tears, a lone eagle spread its broad wings and glided through the air. Dilah rested his head on his paws. He was so sleepy, and he didn't feel cold any more. He drifted.

After a few moments of peace, he was interrupted by a voice.

'What's the matter, lonely little fox?' It was the eagle he had seen in the sky, now perched on a dead tree nearby. 'I wouldn't recommend stopping here.'

'Why?' Dilah asked, yawning.

'Well, as you can see – there are no plants and animals around, only bitter winds, ice and snow. Any creature who rests here is bound to freeze or starve to death. Trust me, I've seen it all.'

'I've been walking for days. I'm tired and hungry. All I want is to sleep for a while.' Dilah's eyes were already growing heavy. 'Why can't you just leave me alone?' he muttered.

'If you close your eyes, you'll never wake up,' the eagle warned. 'Where were you on your way to, anyway?'

'I have a quest . . . a dream, I guess,' Dilah said.

'Well, that settles it! If you have an unfulfilled dream, you must keep going. You can't give up.' The eagle's words struck a chord with Dilah. What was he thinking? His mama had sent him on this quest. He could never give up.

He blinked several times, stood up and shook out his snowy tail.

'Can you tell me where I can find some food?' Dilah asked.

'That's the spirit! The mountains are blocking the warm currents of spring. On the other side, everything's in full bloom. If you can make it across the mountains, you'll survive.'

Dilah surveyed the never-ending chain of snow-capped mountains – towering over the horizon like white giants standing shoulder to shoulder.

The eagle launched himself off the tree and into the blue sky. As he flew off, he called back at Dilah: 'Hurry, white fox! And remember: if you have faith, nothing can stand in your way.'

Soon, the eagle had disappeared into the distance.

Dilah glanced down at the moonstone on his chest, coaxed some movement into his tired limbs, and started running. 'Everything's in full bloom on the other side of those mountains,' he told himself, remembering the eagle's promise. 'Things are looking up.'

Spirits lifted, hope and courage bolstering his heart, he gritted his teeth to stave off hunger and darted toward the snowy mountains, leaving a fresh trail in the snow.

After a while, a shape appeared in the sky – the eagle? Dilah paused and squinted . . . yes, the eagle was returning. A ringing, joyous cry erupted across the mountains as he dropped something from his claws. It landed in front of Dilah, who sniffed at it curiously. A frozen mouse. Dilah's heart surged with warmth. He devoured it in one gulp. It wasn't much, but it might just be enough to keep him alive. The eagle soared towards the mountains, leading the way.

When Dilah reached the foothills, he looked up. The lofty, jagged peaks rose high into the sky. The eagle remained, flying higher and higher. Dilah wished he had wings too – but instead, he struggled on between the endless rocks, feeling like he'd been running for hundreds of years. Finally, the eagle circled high in the sky, and Dilah found himself perched atop the mountain peak. He gazed into the distance, transfixed by the view.

A green forest stretched down the slopes – tall conifers and broad-leaved trees, droplet-laced branches glittering in the sun. At the end of the forest, a beautiful emerald lake shimmered with golden light, reflecting the lush green trees like a magic mirror. Beyond that, a tiny village nestled in a hollow, dotted with small mud-yellow homes and tidy patches of crops basking in the sun.

'Wow!' Dilah marvelled. He'd never seen anything quite like it. He only wished he had someone to share it with.

The eagle screeched overhead, then wheeled away into the blue.

'Thank you!' Dilah called up to the black spot in the sky as it drifted away, feeling his spirits lift.

He bounded down the mountain, the heavy moonstone swaying with each step. By the time he made it to the bottom, it was early evening. Beams of sunlight streaked the horizon, trailing fiery red light between the trees. Small animals scuttled in the undergrowth. Dilah's stomach growled. He darted through the forest, sniffing for something to eat.

It wasn't long before he caught a scent – a scrumptious one. His mouth watered and he rushed off in pursuit.

He slowed his pace and crouched low in the undergrowth as the scent grew stronger. In the afterglow of the sunset, he spotted a small furry creature. The animal was struggling to haul something through the fallen leaves of the forest floor. Dilah inched closer and finally got a better look at him: he had a pair of watery black eyes, two tiny ears that poked up, thin black paws, a yellow back and white belly, and, as well as the delicious-smelling sack, he was lugging around a huge tail that was almost as long as his body. A weasel!

The weasel was so focused on trying to drag his sack that he didn't even notice the white fox watching him from the trees. Dilah had an idea that he couldn't resist! He crept up close to the weasel, puffed up his fur to its fullest height and – jumping out in front of him – shouted, 'Boo!'

The weasel dropped his bag, screeching loudly. His eyes widened as he took in the fearsome fluffy fox. Dilah snarled, baring his teeth. The weasel promptly plopped down on the leaves and played dead.

Dilah burst out laughing.

The weasel furtively opened one eye and looked around. When he caught sight of Dilah giggling nearby, he snapped his eye shut.

'Stop faking. You didn't even faint,' Dilah said, unable to stop laughing completely. 'Look, I'm sorry I frightened you. I just couldn't resist!'

The weasel blinked doubtfully. 'So . . . you're not going to eat me?'

'Nah! But on the subject of food – is there anything to eat in here?' Dilah sniffed the bulging cloth bag and licked his lips. 'I'm starving.'

The weasel's eyes narrowed, but he nodded. 'Of course, if you don't mind what's inside. *Bon appétit!*'

Dilah tipped up the bag, and a handful of round and shiny green things rolled out. He'd never seen this kind of food before.

'What are these?' he asked the weasel, sniffing suspiciously.

'Apples! Haven't you tried one before?'

Dilah shook his head and took a bite. The apple was crisp and tasted both sweet and sour. Delicious! He began gobbling them up, occasionally glancing up at the weasel. A curious expression passed over his face as he watched Dilah eat with such relish. Moments later, the fruit was gone.

'Yum! That was delicious!' Dilah smacked his lips. 'Thank you!'

'My pleasure,' the weasel said through gritted teeth. He rubbed his paws together in front of his chest and forced a smile.

'I'm Dilah. I'm from the Arctic. You?'

'Ankel. I live here,' the weasel replied. 'Now, I really should be getting home.'

Dilah could tell he'd upset the weasel by eating the fruit, even though he'd said it was all right. 'Ankel, I'm sorry about frightening you, and I'm sorry about eating your – your delicious . . .'

'Apples,' Ankel said.

'Apples! Yes. I'm sorry, but if not for your apples, I might've starved to death!'

'Eat up, eat up. Why should I care? It's not like I had to bend over backwards to get them or anything. Yup, they sure are tasty.'

'Where'd they come from?'

Ankel grinned and whispered, 'Don't tell Mum, but I stole them from a hunter's house.'

Dilah gasped, his heart nearly leaping out of his throat. *Hunter?* 'There are h-hunters here?' Dilah stammered. Hunters had killed his parents . . .

Ankel's eyes glinted as Dilah's ears flattened in fear. 'Oh yes! Not just hunters, but also hunting dogs,' he said eagerly. 'Mum says they help hunters find animals who are hiding. They have sensitive noses. It doesn't matter where you hide – they can track your scent. Hunters here like collecting animal fur. I've seen snow leopard skins, rabbit skins, and *fox* skins, as well as—'

'Please stop!' The more Dilah listened to Ankel, the more terrified he felt.

Ankel drew himself up tall, suddenly

emboldened. 'Mum says it's wrong to bully animals who are smaller and weaker. I think you're a thief who targets little animals. You stole my apples.' Ankel glanced at the empty bag on the ground.

Dilah's fear suddenly evaporated. 'I'm not a thief!' he said indignantly. 'You gave me permission.'

'That's, that's because—'

'And if your mama taught you bullying is wrong, didn't she teach you that lying is also wrong?'

Ankel's face reddened beneath his fur.

'Besides,' Dilah said, 'I've already said sorry for eating all the apples, and thanked you for saving me from starvation! If anyone's been rude, it's *you*.'

Eventually, the weasel shook his head. 'A squirrel ran off with a nut I'd just gathered, and then a sparrow flew off with a strawberry I'd just picked, and then this – I'm so unlucky today!' He let out a long breath, his body like a deflated balloon.

'I can help you find other tasty treats – how

does that sound?' Dilah suggested.

'All right. You offered. You'd better keep your word,' Ankel said, managing a smile – and Dilah knew he was forgiven. It was late now, and bright moonlight washed over the forest like a waterfall. 'Arctic fox, why'd you come all the way here?' Ankel asked.

'Call me Dilah.'

'All right. Dilah, why'd you come here?' Before Dilah could figure out how to reply, Ankel clapped his paws. 'You don't have to answer. I already know. You wanted to escape that bloody Arctic winter, didn't you?' He raised a paw to his mouth. 'Oops! Mum doesn't like it when I say bad words.'

'Ankel? Ankel? Is that you?' a voice called out from somewhere nearby.

'Uh-oh! That's her. I'd forgotten the time!' There was a sudden uneasiness in Ankel's eyes. 'Mum – I'm over here!'

The branches of a shrub rattled and a middle-aged weasel stepped out, glaring at Ankel angrily.

'How many times have I told you to come

home before the sun goes down? Do you have any idea how worried I've been? Don't you realize how dangerous it is out here after dark? You could come across a hunter, or a wolf,' she said. Ankel lowered his head. 'Or a-a-a f-f-fox?' As soon as she'd caught sight of Dilah, Ankel's mother had started stuttering.

'Dilah, this is my mum, Azalea,' Ankel started. 'Mum, this is—'

'Ankel, get behind me – now!' Azalea glowered at Dilah as though he were the enemy. He sat neatly, with his tail curled around his paws, and cocked his head to one side.

'Mum, don't be like this. He's a friend. We've just been talking.'

A friend! Dilah's heart lifted.

'No fox is going to *tell* you he has ill intentions. Get over here now! Did you hear me? We're going home.' She turned her burning glare on Dilah. 'And as for you, stay away from my son.'

'I'm sorry, Dilah. My mum is always on high alert,' Ankel said to Dilah as he prepared to leave.

'It's OK,' Dilah said, smiling. What mother didn't look out for her child?

Ankel obediently followed Azalea out of the clearing, words drifting back to Dilah through the quiet night.

'How could you spend all evening chatting with a fox? It's so late! Didn't it occur to you that he could kill you at any time? It's not normal for an Arctic fox to be here!' The sound of Azalea reprimanding her son grew softer, eventually fading away, leaving Dilah all alone.

He thought of his mother, his heart aching. If only Mama were to show up and give him a stern lecture, he would be the happiest fox in the world . . .

Moonlight sifted through the leaves, casting mottled white shadows on the ground that were as milky as pearls. Dilah removed the moonstone from his neck, searched for a relatively empty patch of grass, and opened the leather parcel. The moonstone shone with its mysterious blue light. The small, golden crescent moon in the centre began to glow again, spinning and spinning until it finally stopped at a fixed point, drawing him further south-east. But Dilah knew he wasn't strong enough to carry on just yet.

He found a comfortable hollow at the foot of a tree and sprawled out on the leaves. These past few days had worn him out so much that he fell asleep as soon as he closed his eyes.

The next morning, Dilah was awakened by birdsong. He blinked, his eyes heavy with sleep, and saw magpies perched on the branches above him, chirping loudly as they tended to their nests. He stood up and shook his body. After the apples, and a good night's sleep, he felt stronger than he had in a long time. The sun had already climbed partway over the forest, bathing the earth in warm light.

Dilah decided he'd spend some time here, gathering his strength after the difficult journey across the mountain pass. As he trotted through the forest, he caught a whiff of Ankel's scent. Following it, he found Ankel's home close by – half of a large, dead tree trunk that looked like a giant bone sticking out of the underbrush. There was a small hole in the tangled roots, extremely narrow and surrounded by vines. Only one weasel would be able to enter or exit at a time. As Dilah approached, Azalea was sauntering toward the hole, carrying a pinch of straw in her mouth. She noticed Dilah and froze in surprise, then glared at him, as though she thought he was preparing for an ambush.

Azalea was about to duck inside the den when a tiny yellow head popped out to see what was going on.

'Mum, you're finally home! Did you bring breakfast?' Ankel asked.

'Get inside! That rascal's dropped by!' Azalea snapped.

Ankel followed his mother's gaze. When he saw Dilah, his face lit up.

'Hey, Dilah,' Ankel called out.

Dilah opened his mouth to greet Ankel, but didn't get a chance.

'Get in, get in! Hurry on inside! Don't let the rascal look at you!' Azalea ordered. But Ankel clearly didn't want to go back inside. He didn't budge.

'Didn't you hear me?' Azalea asked.

'But – but—'

'There are no buts. Don't fall for his tricks!'

Ankel drew himself up tall. 'But I'm grown up, Mum; I'm practically an adult. I know right from wrong. Other weasels my age have already left their parents and are living on their own. And I want to be friends with—'

'Child, you're still young and naive. The outside world is full of danger. I'm worried you'll have a hard time on your own. I want you to stay with me so I can take care of you.' It sounded to Dilah as though Azalea spoke from the bottom of her heart.

Ankel reluctantly lowered himself back inside the log. Although he understood why Azalea wanted to protect her son, Dilah felt angry at her. Why wouldn't she give him a chance? He hadn't done anything wrong. He liked Ankel and he happened to be a fox – what was wrong with that?

*

Over the next few days, Dilah stayed nearby. He rested and feasted on mushrooms and felt himself grow stronger, but Azalea's prejudice towards him only increased. She kept Ankel inside as much possible, and when he did go out, she watched him like a hawk. If they ran into Dilah, she'd quickly lead Ankel away, although Ankel would shoot him apologetic glances over his shoulder. Gradually, Dilah realized that Azalea's love for her son was keeping him trapped. Until Ankel left home, he'd never be free.

One bright and beautiful morning, Dilah was wandering through the forest when he caught a whiff of something strange – it wasn't a weasel, nor was it any of the other small creatures who lived in the forest. What was it? He followed the scent for a while before realizing he'd reached the path that led to Ankel's home. As he drew close he caught a whiff of blood and his heart started to beat faster. Was Ankel's family in danger? He slowed down, tiptoeing among the trees. After a while, he heard movement. Through the leaves, he saw something that made his heart rise to his throat: a huge snow leopard standing beneath a tree, a cold, murderous glint in its eyes. Across from him, a timid animal lay on its back, trembling from head to toe: Ankel.

Azalea rarely let Ankel go out – what was he doing outside so early in the morning? What would happen if Dilah tried to rescue Ankel? The snow leopard was a sleek, muscled killer: Dilah would die if he tried to fight it. He hesitated as the leopard slowly closed in on the weasel, clearly enjoying toying with its prey.

Just then, a loud voice rang out.

'Ankel – Ankel – where are you?' Azalea angrily called. She continued, muttering to herself: 'I can't believe he slipped out while I was asleep! When will he learn? I told him to stay away from that fox. He's up to no good—'

Azalea emerged from the undergrowth and froze at the sight before her.

'Ankel!' she screamed. Azalea didn't hesitate for more than a second: she threw herself between Ankel and the snow leopard. Holding out her paws, she used her own body to shield her son's. She was frightened out of her mind, yet brave enough to risk her own life to save her child.

'I'm begging you! Please don't eat my child!' Azalea pleaded. 'Eat me instead! I have more meat on me!'

'Scram, old weasel!' the snow leopard snarled. 'I like my meat tender!' He crept towards the weasels, growling. His burning orange eyes were fixed on Ankel, who was hiding behind his mother.

'Eat me instead! I'm begging you! Have mercy – he's still young. Let him go!' Azalea cried.

'Didn't you hear me? Get lost!' The snow leopard licked his lips, expressionless, ready to lunge at Ankel. 'Or I'll kill you first and eat him next . . .'

Dilah glimpsed his own mother in Azalea: she too would've charged forward to protect him, without thinking about herself. He couldn't let this happen! The leopard bared its teeth and Dilah sensed it was about to pounce . . .

'You're the one who should get lost!' Dilah

shouted, leaping out of his hiding place and snarling fiercely at the big cat, who was three times his size.

The snow leopard turned around to face Dilah, who tried very hard not to tremble under his fiery stare.

'Let them go, you big cowardly cat!' Dilah demanded, his voice quavering slightly.

'Oh? So you're volunteering to take their place?' The snow leopard narrowed his eyes. 'Fox, being a busybody can kill you . . .'

'I'm not afraid of you!' Dilah squeaked. Peering past the leopard, he silently willed Azalea and Ankel to run – but Azalea was frozen in shock, her eyes fixed on the spot where the leopard had been standing moments ago. Ankel had disappeared, perhaps to fetch help.

'You're not afraid of me? Then what on earth *are* you afraid of?' the snow leopard asked, sounding a little offended.

'Umm . . .' Dilah racked his brains for the most ferocious animal in the world. Glancing past the leopard, he noticed that Azalea, too, had now disappeared. He felt a surge of relief, but couldn't help hoping the two weasels hadn't left him to die . . .

'Well? Can't think of a more fearsome creature than me?' the leopard said in a superior tone. 'I thought not.'

'Polar bears!' Dilah blurted. 'Even you must be scared of those.'

The snow leopard scoffed. 'You think I'm afraid of a big silly lug like a polar bear? Let me tell you, the only animal I fear in this world is the hunter! Now, enough of this. I'm hungry.'

The snow leopard charged at Dilah and everything slowed down. The leopard's front and back legs took turns forcefully gripping the ground, his thick paws stirring up clouds of dead leaves. His long tail was raised high and the lines of his silhouette were graceful and angular. He kicked hard and leapt through the air, and Dilah had a heartbeat to snap out of his trance-like state and leap aside. His own body felt sluggish, but he did it: feeling the heat of the leopard's body ruffling against his fur. The snow leopard growled and swiped at Dilah with his huge paw, claws out like tiny knives.

Dilah jumped aside again, dodging the claws by a whisker. The leopard roared, a murderous fire in his eyes.

Dilah ran.

The snow leopard was faster, but Dilah was small and nimble. He ducked behind a tall pine on instinct. The snow leopard sprang to the left of the trunk; Dilah ran to the right. The leopard chased Dilah to the right, and Dilah went left, running circles around the tree. Losing patience, the snow leopard scaled the tree trunk and peered down at Dilah with narrowed, triumphant eyes.

Before Dilah could move, the snow leopard leapt from above, crushing Dilah beneath his paws.

Dilah desperately fought to break free. He knew exactly what would happen next: the snow leopard's pointed fangs would pierce his throat . . . He felt his heart pounding beneath the leopard's paw. He thought of his mama and papa and he squeezed his eyes shut, waiting to die, feeling the moonstone's weight around his neck. But death didn't come: the snow leopard was oddly still. Dilah opened his eyes. The animal's ears had perked up, straining to make out a noise in the distance.

It was a dog's bark. The snow leopard studied the dense trees, panic sweeping through his eyes.

'Hunter . . . ?' the leopard whispered.

Woof woof, woof! The barks grew louder. The snow leopard lifted his weight slightly from Dilah's chest, claws retracting.

'Hunter! Run!' a familiar voice shouted.

The snow leopard shivered and jumped away from Dilah, who scrambled to his feet, unsteady but unharmed. Drooling, the snow leopard eyed him, reluctant to let his prey escape, but he chose to preserve his own life. He spun around and vanished into the trees.

Dilah released a deep breath. His heart was still thumping hard but his legs were trembling – he couldn't run. Where was the hunter? He had to hide!

'Dilah!' It was Ankel, his head popping out from behind a tree. He was smiling. Dilah frowned – what was so funny? Then Ankel barked . . . and Dilah understood: the barking hadn't come from a hunting dog at all, but from Ankel! Azalea was the one who'd shouted 'Hunter!' She emerged from behind the tree, glancing nervously around the clearing, as if she expected the snow leopard to return at any moment.

Ankel walked over to Dilah. Despite his smile, he was clearly shaken.

'Thank you!' Dilah and Ankel said to each other at the same time.

'Ankel – Ankel – my child!' Azalea rushed forward, hugging Ankel tightly. 'My darling – I was worried to death – I thought we . . . I love you very, very much.' Her eyes were full of tears. Dilah felt a tug in his own throat and lowered his gaze.

'It's OK, Mum. It's all right,' Ankel patted Azalea's back.

Azalea glanced up at Dilah. 'What a brave fox! I doubted you before, but today you stepped forward and saved us both! How can I ever thank you?'

'No . . . thank *you*,' Dilah said, feeling a little

bashful. 'If you and Ankel hadn't driven away the snow leopard, I'd be in his stomach by now.'

'If you hadn't distracted him in the first place, I'd have been torn to pieces!' Ankel cut in.

'Ankel's right. You saved us first,' said Azalea, smiling. 'Now, I think we could all use some breakfast, couldn't we?' She turned back towards the hollow trunk, leaving Dilah and Ankel alone in the clearing.

'You were great!' Dilah said to Ankel. 'You scared away the snow leopard – it was amazing! How did you know what to do?'

'It's no big deal. It was a piece of cake.' Ankel smiled bashfully. 'The snow leopard himself told us how to make him go away. He said: "The only animal I fear in this world is the hunter." I've heard a hunting dog tons of times and I knew I could do a good impression.'

'When I heard the barking, I really thought it was a hunting dog!'

They made their way back to the den, and just as they arrived, Azalea emerged, carrying a mountain of food in her arms: bunches of carrots, wild mushrooms, a couple of fish caught from the lake, and even a few shiny clumps of algae. 'Breakfast time,' she announced, placing the feast on the ground between the two friends. 'Tuck in!'

Dilah and Ankel spent the whole day playing and chatting, until Azalea called her son to bed. Dilah settled down nearby, tired after the day's excitement – but as he was falling asleep, he heard soft footsteps – the rustling of paws on fallen leaves. Opening his eyes, he found a pile of nuts in front of him.

He looked around curiously. He saw a fluffy ball of

yellow creeping away, back to the hollow tree trunk, as if afraid of waking him up.

'Ankel?'

The little weasel stopped and glanced back, smiling. 'I gathered those in the forest. I've been saving them a long time. I hope you'll enjoy them.'

A feeling of warmth washed over Dilah.

CHAPTER 5

Sneaking Food

The next morning, Ankel asked Azalea if he could go play with Dilah again. After rattling off a long list of things to watch out for, Azalea agreed. Ankel told Dilah he wanted to show him a special place, somewhere that was both exciting and filled with tasty treats. Dilah only half believed him.

They walked in the direction of the rising sun. After a while, they emerged from the forest. They passed the emerald-coloured lake Dilah had seen from the mountaintop, the clear ripples glimmering. A team of ducks floated on the surface, and a few cows stood at the edge, drinking the water.

Gradually, small earthen houses sprang into view, one after another, rows of crops neatly lined up behind them. Dilah stopped and looked around anxiously.

'Why'd you stop?' Ankel asked, glancing back.

'How . . . how could you bring me to a place where there are humans?' Dilah's voice trembled with fear. He was beginning to regret coming out with Ankel. The memory of all that had passed with the woodsman and his family was still fresh in his mind.

'Are you scared? The place I was talking about is around here,' Ankel said, completely unconcerned.

'*Here?*' Dilah repeated. He felt his hackles rise and swished his tail uneasily. 'I wouldn't dream of going inside a place where humans gather. Not any more.'

'Don't worry, Dilah. It's a small trail and well hidden. No humans will see us,' Ankel said confidently. 'C'mon, this way. Keep up with me!' He leapt into a field of low crops.

Dilah didn't want to end up lost, so he reluctantly followed his friend.

'Keep your head down,' Ankel whispered as they weaved through fields, hiding beneath the tall plants.

Chickens clucked nearby and Dilah nearly jumped out of his fur when he heard a dog barking. He could smell humans nearby now, and he shivered in fear. Dilah and Ankel pushed through a tall bush, lurking in its shadow. Ankel clearly knew his way around. A few moments later, he led Dilah to the side of a small earthen house. Dilah heaved a deep sigh, trying to calm his pounding heart.

'We're here!' Ankel cheerfully announced.

Dilah sized up the mud-yellow structure. It looked similar to the other earthen houses in the area. The only difference was that various animal skins hung from frames in the yard: wolf skins, mink skins, rabbit skins, as well as numerous other skins that he didn't recognize. He was in no mood to find out. His heart thumped ever harder against his chest as frightening smells assaulted his nose – smells of blood and fear.

'What is this place?' Dilah asked.

'A hunter's house, of course,' Ankel calmly answered.

'Are you crazy?' Dilah stepped back in horror. 'How could you—'

'Don't be afraid, Dilah,' the weasel said. 'Do you remember the first time we met? You asked me where those apples came from – well, I'd stolen them from this hunter's house. I had an unforgettable feast here. Words can't even begin to describe all of the scrumptious things I ate in this special place. We must try our luck today!'

Ankel's definition of a 'special place' was very different from Dilah's. He'd rather sit down to dinner with Carl and the blue foxes than stay here one second longer.

'Ankel, we're going to get ourselves killed. Take me back!' Dilah hissed.

But Ankel waved a paw dismissively. 'We're here now, so we might as well look for a bite to eat! Besides, the hunter's not home during the day – trust me. The only one home is that pesky dog. Look, I'll go in and find us some food. All you have to do is stand guard,' Ankel said breezily.

'What? There's a dog? A *hunting* dog?' Dilah was even more afraid now.

'Of course! Didn't I say I'd heard it loads of times?' Ankel pointed. 'Look, there he is. He's called Toby.' Dilah peeked around the side of the house, into the front garden. Sure enough, he spotted a hunting dog lying against the door of the earthen house. The dog had a shaggy grey coat. It was huge: about the size of the snow leopard, with a thick chain hanging around its neck.

Ankel appeared to read the terror on Dilah's face, because he softened his tone. 'Listen, Dilah, you just hide right here in this tall grass, and keep an eye out for anyone who comes towards the house.'

'What should I do if someone comes?' Dilah asked.

'That's easy. Do what I did yesterday – bark

like a dog to warn me. That way, they won't get suspicious. When I hear your warning, I'll escape through the back window. But don't worry – no one will come.'

A vivid picture formed in Dilah's mind: a hunter discovering a fox hiding in the tall grass outside his home, barking his fool head off like a dog. He stared at Ankel in disbelief.

Ankel continued, 'One more thing. If you have an accident or come across something dangerous, don't worry about me. Run away. Got it?'

'What about you?'

'Relax. I've been here loads of times.' Ankel crept toward the house. 'Good luck. See you soon!'

Ankel tiptoed right by the sleeping hound. Sensing movement, the dog opened his eyes and saw the weasel. He snarled and tugged at his chain, kicking up clouds of dust. But Ankel walked on, just outside the reach of the chain. The dog couldn't get to him.

'Hush, Toby!' Ankel ordered, with a sparkle in his eye.

This made Toby even angrier. He growled louder, and strained against the chain until it was close to choking him. His bloodshot eyes bulged with the effort, but he couldn't even reach one of Ankel's paws. The dog barked furiously. Ankel smirked at Toby, deftly climbed on to a grain sack resting against the wall, and squeezed through the little window beside the door. Dilah anxiously waited out of sight, his heart pounding.

A moment later, the young fox heard footsteps approaching. He peered out over the tall grass, his stomach doing somersaults, his fur standing up. A middle-aged man was heading for the house, a sack slung over his shoulder. He had curly brown hair and a steely gaze, and he was wearing a thick coat and sturdy boots. Dilah felt a flash of anger. Ankel had promised this wouldn't happen! But the anger was quickly drowned by terror. He knew first-hand how cruel humans could be – what would the hunter do to Ankel if he found him? *I can't let that happen!*

Dilah pulled himself together and took a

deep breath. '*Woof woof! Woof, woof woof woof!*' he yelped. But that pesky hound was barking too – how was Ankel supposed to hear? Dilah's attempts were completely drowned out by the big dog's.

'Toby, what's wrong?' the hunter asked his dog, heading for the wooden door to the house.

Toby barked up at his owner.

'Did you see something, boy?' the hunter said, setting down his bag. 'Let's see . . .'

No! Dilah thought, panicking.

The man fished out a key from his pocket and unlocked the wooden door. He went straight inside and slammed it shut.

I have to do something!

Dilah leapt out of the grass and shouted at the top of his lungs: 'Ankel, run!'

As soon as Toby spotted Dilah, he stopped barking. A second later, he howled. A few seconds passed: no response from the house. The dog growled at Dilah and howled a second time.

'Ankel!' Dilah called again, creeping closer. 'Get out!'

Toby howled a third time, and the wooden door flung open. Holding on to the handle with one hand, the hunter stuck out his head and yelled, 'Shut up, Toby! My head's exploding!'

Obeying his master's orders, Toby fell silent. The door slammed shut. Panting, Toby glared at Dilah. Dilah paced back and forth at the edge of the yard, wondering if the hunter had found Ankel – had killed him. If Ankel didn't return home, how would he explain it to Azalea?

A yellow speck on the chimney caught Dilah's attention. It grew larger and larger, twisting this way and that. He squinted, then realized it was Ankel's head poking out and scanning the area. The weasel wriggled out of the chimney, a rope of pink sausages coiled around his neck. The weight on Dilah's chest lifted, and he smiled in relief.

Ankel carefully crawled down the sloping roof so that the sausages wouldn't slip off his neck. When he reached the lowest point, he nimbly leapt on to a water butt, slid down its side and landed on the ground.

'Bravo!' Dilah said. 'Now – let's get out of here!'

'Agreed,' Ankel replied.

Dilah followed Ankel back towards the fields, Toby barking and howling as they disappeared into the tall grass. After a few moments, they heard the hunter roar, 'Toby! What's wrong with you? If you don't shut up, I'm going to throw you out!'

Dilah and Ankel scampered through the

grassy fields until they left the village safely behind. At last, they found a quiet hillside near the lake and sprawled out in the sun, laughing in relief.

'We got lucky today!' Ankel lifted up the delicious-smelling sausages with his tiny paw.

'Lucky? That was a really close call! How'd you get out?' Dilah asked. 'Did you hear my warning signal?'

'Of course not. Toby's barking was a hundred times louder than yours,' Ankel said. 'When I heard Toby still barking after I'd gone inside, I knew we were in trouble. I realized it'd draw attention.'

'So how'd you get out from under the hunter's nose?' Dilah asked, settling his chin on his paws.

'As soon as I got inside, I made a beeline for the kitchen and started rummaging for food. When the hunter opened the door, I hid behind a basket. He took a quick look, then went to nap on the sofa. I rummaged a bit more before I found the sausages. At that point, it wasn't practical to go out the window, so I crawled into the chimney and climbed out. Even though things didn't go quite as planned, we still pulled it off.'

'*You* pulled it off. You really have a knack for stealing!' Dilah said.

'Yup.' Ankel sat up straight on the grass and met Dilah's eyes. 'By the way,' he said solemnly, 'please don't tell my mum about today. She'll only worry.'

'Of course I won't.'

The little weasel relaxed, his sparkling eyes drifting towards the pile of sausages. 'I bet you've never had anything like this before. Let's eat!'

Dilah and Ankel divided up the stolen sausages and devoured them. It was the best thing Dilah had ever tasted. Human food was so delicious! *When I'm human*, Dilah thought, feeling the weight of the moonstone around his neck, *I'll eat sausages all the time*.

Stuffed, Dilah and Ankel sunbathed on the hill. A gentle breeze blew, the treetops swayed, and the soft sunlight flowed over the grass like melting ice cream. Dilah felt as if he might drift off to sleep.

'Dilah, tell me a story,' Ankel said. 'I've been going on and on about myself these past couple of days, but you're still a mystery to me.'

'I . . .' Dilah was tongue-tied. Where should he start? The past few weeks rushed through his mind. Suddenly, he didn't feel so sleepy.

'Tell me about your family. Why are you here by yourself?'

'My parents are gone,' Dilah said matter-of-factly.

'Oh, I'm so sorry!' Ankel blurted. 'What I mean is . . . what happened?'

'A hunter killed them.'

'Oh!' Ankel sounded shocked. He placed a small paw in front of his mouth and nibbled nervously on his claw. 'No wonder you're so afraid of hunters. But why did you come here? Does it have something to do with that thing around your neck?'

'How did you know?'

'The first time I saw you, I knew you were no ordinary fox. Apparently, there's a wasteland on the other side of the mountain. Even an animal as strong as a snow leopard wouldn't dare set foot over the pass. But you came from the north, somewhere even farther away, and a million times colder. You must have gone through so much, more than I can ever imagine,' Ankel said. 'Now, as to your little parcel, I couldn't help noticing that you've never taken it off, no matter what. It seems more valuable to you than your own life. What is this object that you'll risk your life to protect? It must be something very special. Something powerful enough to send you miles and miles from your home. Or maybe you'd rather not say . . .'

Dilah removed the parcel from his neck and set it down on the grass, carefully opening it. The stone sat on the grass, a blaze flickering merrily at its heart, casting blue flecks of light all around it. Time stopped. Ankel couldn't stop staring at the moonstone, his eyes as wide as saucers.

'Wow, it's incredible! It's so beautiful . . .' Ankel blinked. 'What is it?'

'It's called a moonstone. My mama left it for me.'

'It doesn't look like an ordinary gem. That

blue fire . . . How'd your mum end up with it?'

Dilah paused for a moment, unsure how to answer. 'Ankel, what do you think of humans?' he asked eventually.

'I don't have any particular opinion of them. The people in the village don't take much notice of us – and we don't take much notice of them. Well, except to steal food, sometimes.' He winked at Dilah. 'But mostly, we get along as neighbours.'

'Do you envy them?'

'Of course! The promise of human food is enough to make me risk breaking into the hunter's home – imagine if you could eat it all the time! And don't even get me started on their lives. They rule the world, do whatever they please,' Ankel said, his voice filled with longing. 'They have comfortable, warm homes. They don't have to worry about being eaten – instead, wild animals keep away from them. But what I envy most of all is their endless books and knowledge.'

'If you could become human, would you do it?'

'How? Animals are animals. Humans are humans.'

'But what if you could? I said *if*.' Dilah was eager to hear Ankel's answer.

'Then yes! I'd want to be a scholar and make my mum proud of me.' Ankel smiled. 'But Dilah, what does this have to do with the moonstone?'

'In the Arctic, the patron saint of the white foxes is named Ulla. Legend has it that a long time ago, he created a secret treasure that can turn animals into humans.'

'No way! That's not possible – it's just a myth.' Ankel shook his head.

'My mother told me this secret just before she died, and she gave me the moonstone to lead me to it. So I believe it.' Dilah met Ankel's eyes until the weasel lowered his gaze.

'Can it really be true?'

Dilah gently nodded, gazing at the ducks playing on the lake. The breeze ruffled his fur. He felt a kinship with Ankel that he couldn't explain.

'But how has the legend brought you here, Dilah?' Ankel asked.

Dilah took a deep breath. 'It all started when my parents were killed,' he began. And bit by bit, he told Ankel the story of how he had come to be in the forest – he told him of the blue foxes, of Egg the seal, of how they cracked the code of the moonstone, of his journey south and all that had befallen the human family in the other woods, far away, and, at last, of his journey over the treacherous mountain pass, and the friendly eagle who had guided his way. It had been a long and lonely journey, he realized, and the thought of setting out again alone made his heart heavy. 'And you know the rest,' Dilah finished. 'So that's how I ended up here.'

Ankel was quiet for a moment. He clearly didn't know what to make of it all.

'Ankel . . .' Dilah had trouble getting the words out, as though there was a fishbone stuck in his throat. 'Do you . . . do you want to help me look for the treasure?'

'Me?' Dumbfounded, Ankel pointed to himself and frowned. 'I . . . I don't know, Dilah. Can I think about it?'

Dilah was glad Ankel hadn't said 'no' outright. 'Of course. Along the way, we'll face terrible danger. We might get lost or get ill, get caught by humans, freeze to death, starve to death, or even be eaten by wild animals . . .' With each phrase, Ankel's tiny eyes widened in alarm. 'But at least we'd be together. And then, at the end, I think we could really do it. I think we could really become human.'

'Become . . . human.' Ankel appeared to test out the words, his voice slow and wondering. Then he hesitated. 'But Dilah, are humans really as perfect as we imagine?'

'What do you mean?'

'I mean, is it really worth all the trouble?' Ankel asked.

Dilah had felt this doubt niggling him before, especially after the murder of Leo's parents, but he'd tried to squash it down. Surely the quest his mother had sent him on couldn't be a fool's errand? He looked at Ankel and asked, 'What do you mean?'

'Well . . . although humans rule the natural world, they don't seem to value each other's lives, do they? After what happened to Mideo and Lily . . . and all for a few tree trunks . . .' Ankel shook his head. 'Are you sure you want to be like those men?'

Dilah thought about this carefully, but eventually he nodded. 'Yes. They don't represent *all* humans. Remember how kind Mideo and Lily were to me? There are good humans and bad humans, just like there are good foxes and bad foxes.' Dilah paused to compose his thoughts further. 'Besides, if I do end up succeeding, I wouldn't be a bad human. In fact, being a human means I'd have more power to stop the bad people, like the ones who killed Mideo and Lily.' He would never forget how it had felt to sit in the shadows and watch the couple die. *If I'd been human, maybe I could have helped.*

'That makes sense . . .' Ankel was rubbing his little paws together anxiously, as though he were struggling to make up his mind. 'It'll be dangerous – that's a given,' he mumbled to himself. 'Mum won't like it, but I think we can make it . . .' He raised his head and clapped his paws. 'I'm in.'

'Really?' Dilah yelped.

Little Ankel trembled with excitement. He nodded. 'Yes, really!'

A wonderful realization filled Dilah with warmth until it felt like his heart was glowing – he wouldn't be alone any more! He'd have a friend! 'Will you be ready to leave tomorrow?' he asked Ankel. 'See, I've been here for a while already. According to the moonstone, the treasure is somewhere south, but I don't know how far. The sooner we set out, the better.'

'OK,' Ankel agreed. 'I can't wait! But –' his voice grew suddenly serious – 'there's one thing I have to do before we go, and it isn't going to be easy.'

Dilah nodded, feeling his heart clench on his friend's behalf. 'Tell your mum.'

It was morning. The sun spilled rays of warm, bright light into the forest and birds chirped all around. Dilah waited outside Ankel's family den. After a while, Azalea emerged from the hollow trunk. Her eyes were red and swollen, her face worn. Ankel emerged next – but Dilah almost didn't recognize him: he looked totally grown-up and very neat and tidy. He'd combed the yellow fur on his head so smoothly that not a single hair stood out of place and his little head gleamed in the sun. Not a word was spoken as they set off into the forest.

Accompanied by Azalea, the two friends headed south through the familiar trees. As they reached the edge of the forest, Azalea gripped Ankel's paw.

'Remember not to sleep on wet leaves, or you'll catch a cold,' Azalea warned.

Ankel nodded.

'Promise me you'll eat three meals a day, OK?'

Ankel nodded again.

'You know that if you smell blood, you need to hide, right? Don't travel when it rains – find a cave and take cover.'

Ankel nodded mechanically.

'Also, you must avoid humans, especially hunters. Do you remember?'

Ankel and Dilah exchanged a knowing glance before Ankel said, 'Yes, Mum.'

'Oh, and bathe yourself once a week, or you'll get fleas.'

Ankel was becoming impatient.

'Also—' Azalea started to say.

'Mum, Dilah's already been waiting a long time.'

'Just one last thing. My dear, you must take good care of yourself. I'm going to miss you terribly.' Azalea's nose was twitching as if she was trying to stop herself from crying. She and Ankel hugged tightly. 'I'm so proud of you, Ankel,' Dilah heard her whisper in her son's ear. When they finally drew apart, she turned to Dilah.

'Please look after him, Dilah.' Tears swirled in her eyes, but she didn't let them fall.

'Don't worry, we'll look after each other.'

Once their goodbyes were done, Dilah and Ankel turned to the south. A meadow yawned into the distance – beyond it, rolling hills of all sizes bumped across the horizon. As they set off, Dilah didn't look back, afraid to see Azalea's heartbroken face – but Ankel turned and waved several times until they were too far away to see the little weasel among the trees.

'Are you ready for our adventure to begin?' asked Dilah.

'I'm ready!' Ankel excitedly replied, his eyes twinkling.

'Then let's go!' Dilah took off running, and Ankel sprinted alongside him. A blur of white and yellow streaked across the green meadow, like three colours splashed across a canvas. How long and far they would have to run was anyone's guess.

CHAPTER 6

The Iron Hooves of Kvik Valley

When night fell, Dilah laid the moonstone on a soft patch of grass and opened the parcel. Ankel watched with great interest. The golden crescent in the middle of the moonstone spun, whirling round and round until it stopped at last, pointing the way forward.

'Wow, it's amazing!' Ankel couldn't believe his eyes. He studied the glowing crescent moon, its golden light beaming on to his face. 'It's like a compass,' he said.

'Compass?'

'A tool invented by humans. The needle always points north. If you have one, you'll never get lost,' Ankel explained.

'Humans are so smart! I've never seen a compass. Maybe it's the same thing as the moonstone.'

'No, this is definitely different.' Ankel's eyes sparkled in the light of the moonstone.

'It's taken me a lot of work to figure out how to use it!'

'Wait – is this the poem you told me about earlier?' Ankel had noticed the script written on the leather.

He picked it up. In the faint moonlight, he carefully studied the verse, mumbling to himself, poring over each and every word. *'When you're lost, let the sky lead the way,'* he murmured at last.

'How can you understand that?' Dilah stared at Ankel in shock, his jaw hanging open. He remembered Grandpa Turtle saying that most of the animals who could read the characters were extinct.

'You mean Classical Animalese?' He chuckled. 'My grandpa taught it to me when I was small. He has a knack for languages.'

'Wow! Did he teach you other stuff about animal history?'

Ankel's ears perked up at Dilah's interest. 'Of course! He told me that animal civilizations developed millions of years ago, earlier than human civilizations. Animals have their own cultures and lifestyles – we all know that. But in the past, our ancestors used pictures and symbols to record their civilizations, just like humans did.'

'Where did they record these things?' Dilah asked.

'On the walls of caves, or on rocks on the seabed – though when humans discovered these strange symbols, they assumed it was the work of other humans . . . or even aliens!'

'But what happened? Why don't we use writing any more?'

'According to Grandpa, humans plundered natural resources and enslaved and killed animals to further their interests, which quickly advanced human civilizations . . . but destroyed animal civilizations. Gradually, the written language stopped being used – and the spoken language evolved into what we speak now: Modern Animalese.'

Dilah was lost in thought. If he became human, even if he was a *good* human, would he hurt and kill animals? If human civilization was founded on enslaving and killing animals, how could he avoid it? He shivered.

'Ankel,' he said at last, 'if we really become human, we must do something to help the animals.'

The next morning, golden rays of sun streamed between the clouds on to the emerald grass, the leaves glistening with dew. Mist drifted over the hills. Dilah and Ankel continued on their way, the scent of wildflowers wafting on the breeze. All colours of petals bloomed in the meadows as far as the eye could see, trailing all the way up to the hills. Spring was well and truly here. Bees hummed among the flowers, and butterflies sunned their wings, flitting into the air as Ankel and Dilah passed.

By afternoon, the clouds had passed and the sky was clear and bright. They'd come upon a vast and magnificent prairie, the rolling hills dotted with herders' huts – although there wasn't a human in sight. Every so often, cattle cried out. White sheep grazed in the glossy green grass. A small stream glittering with sunlight flowed through the prairie, cows standing beside it to take a drink.

When they reached the stream, Dilah too had a drink of water. As he was about to leave, following Ankel further downstream, an unusual detail caught his eye: in the distance, there was a white horse tied to a cypress tree.

As Ankel and Dilah drew closer, the fox noticed how the young horse was standing quietly with her head bowed, tears staining her face.

She was white all over except for black rings around her hooves, a pearl-coloured mane hanging neatly from her neck. Her large, weary eyes were welling up with tears. The horse turned away when she noticed Dilah, clearly not wanting them to see her crying.

'What's wrong?' Dilah asked, gently.

'None of your business!' the horse snapped.

'But why are you crying?'

'I . . .' she started, but shook her head. 'It's too embarrassing.'

'If you don't want to say, then we can't help you. We'll leave you to it,' Dilah said. 'Sorry to

disturb you. Come on, Ankel.' They started to walk away.

'You could help me?' the horse said.

Ankel and Dilah nodded, turning around. 'We can try!' said Ankel.

She sighed loudly. 'I'll tell you, then. I-I was caught by humans . . .' She was so worked up, it was hard for her to talk. 'Zelvia will never forgive me.'

'Who's Zelvia? Wait, sorry – take your time and start from the beginning. What happened?' Dilah asked carefully.

The horse let out a huge sigh. 'Two days ago, my herd was on the move in the Kvik Valley. We were ambushed and surrounded by humans, who wanted to catch some wild horses and tame them. It was total chaos – people on horseback came out of nowhere and started chasing us. Everyone bolted away. The horse behind me knocked me over. As I struggled to get up, all of the my herd ran off, leaving me behind. A man threw a rope around my neck, and they brought me here.'

Dilah remembered what Ankel had told him

about how human civilizations were founded on enslaving animals. 'Were you the only one caught?' he asked.

'No, it was me and Otis. He's too old to run.'

'The young and old are always the target of predators.' Ankel shook his head.

'Where is he now? Is he tied up too?' Dilah asked.

'No. They–they killed him for meat when they realized he was useless.' The young horse burst into tears again.

Dilah swallowed, feeling a lump in his own throat. Another innocent life had been taken by humans.

'I don't know what they're going to do to me next. Sometimes I wish they'd just put me out of my misery. Maybe I'm better off dead,' the young horse said grimly.

'Why?' Dilah asked, confused. 'If we help you escape, you can run back to your herd, can't you?'

'No, that's the thing . . .' The horse glanced down at her hooves, her voice so low that Dilah could barely hear it. 'They put shoes on me – a symbol of shame. My herd will never accept me now.'

'I'm sorry. I don't get it.' Ankel frowned. 'Why are horseshoes so bad?'

'In this world, there are two kinds of horses: domesticated and wild – like me. We're the same species, but we're from two different clans. We might look the same on the outside, but inside we're different. They're tame and weak, while we're strong and independent. Nothing can hold us down,' the horse said solemnly, raising her head. 'We despise them.'

'Because they serve humans?' Ankel asked.

'M-hmm. As soon as a shoe is nailed to a wild horse's hoof, it means she's lost her soul. It's a mark of slavery to humans, a crime that can't ever be scrubbed away. From then on, all wild horses will shun you. Even if you break free, the best you can hope for is to wander alone in the mountains.' The horse dug her hooves into the ground. 'Zelvia is the leader of the wild horses. He hates humans, and hates horses enslaved by humans even more. He'll never forgive me, that's for sure.'

'I see . . .' Dilah said, deep in thought.

'Anyway, can you help me break this rope? I might not be able to go home, but at least I can wander on my own,' the horse said glumly.

'Don't give up so easily,' Dilah said. 'You should go back to the horses, explain the situation to them, and fight for your right to stay.'

'It's a waste of time. Zelvia won't listen to me.'

'In that case, maybe he'll listen to us,' Ankel offered.

'I don't want to get you involved. It could be dangerous for you both.'

'If there's even the slightest glimmer of hope, we should try,' Dilah said, cocking his head. 'Don't you think?'

'Hope? Is there really a glimmer of hope?'

'My friend, there always is,' Dilah said, smiling.

Ankel stood beneath the horse's neck, his two little paws clutching the rope, and bit down with his sharp front teeth. Before long, he had gnawed through it, and the frayed end fell to the ground, as stiff as a dead snake. The horse reared up and neighed with joy, then took off like a flash of lightning, kicking up dust. Dilah and Ankel followed.

'What's your name?' Dilah called out.

'Kassel, a free galloper of the prairie. You guys?'

'I'm Dilah, and this is Ankel,' Dilah panted, the moonstone thumping against his chest.

'Hey! Do you think you could slow down? I'm already . . . running . . . as fast as . . . I can!' Ankel gasped, his short limbs flying off the ground as he lagged behind the others.

Kassel slowed just enough for the others to keep up, and they ran for hours, the scenery gradually changing. The green land grew sparser, replaced by chunks of rocks. Finally, Kassel slowed to a stop, her breathing quickly returning to normal. A few moments later, Dilah and Ankel dropped to the ground beside her, panting heavily. Dilah stuck his tongue out, trying to cool down, while Ankel slumped on his back, his chest heaving.

'I'm home! This is the Kvik Valley,' Kassel said.

'This place is beautiful!' Dilah said between gulping breaths. And it was: the air was hot and dry, the bare yellow earth scorched by the sun, and endless mountain peaks stabbed the azure sky.

'What do you eat?' Ankel managed. 'There's nothing here!' Dilah gazed around at the rocky terrain: he was right, the vegetation was sparse.

'It's not ideal,' said Kassel, shaking out her mane, 'but generally, humans don't come here, so we're safe.'

'Where is your herd?' Dilah asked.

'Usually over that ridge, this time of day,' Kassel said. 'Come with me.'

As they climbed up the slope, Dilah heard a deep rumble, the earth shaking beneath his paws. The sound grew and grew until, as they reached the ridge, a haze billowed from the valley below. Scores of wild horses galloped in the sunlight – white, black, golden, brown – there were at least forty or fifty. Dust flew up around them in a raging tempest and Dilah couldn't imagine anything standing in their way.

Dilah and Ankel heard a loud peal behind them that echoed the voices of the wild horses. They glanced back and saw Kassel standing on her hind legs, her two front legs raised high in the air, neck outstretched towards the sky. Her long, smooth tail swished over them as she jumped. Kassel barrelled down the mountain at an impossible speed, heading for the herd. The other horses stopped when they noticed her speeding toward them. They slowly approached, eyes fixed on the young mare.

Dilah and Ankel hung back as a jet-black horse stepped to the front and stared at Kassel without speaking. The horse's dark coat gleamed in the sun. He had a powerful build – broad chest, sturdy legs – and looked extremely strong. In comparison, Kassel was slight, and Dilah felt suddenly afraid for his new friend. He hoped they had done the right thing in encouraging her to return.

'Kassel?' whispered a yellow horse further back in the herd, as if he couldn't believe his eyes.

'Welcome home, child,' an older brownish-red horse whinnied, smiling.

'Shameless traitor!' a white horse snarled, kicking furiously at the ground and glaring at Kassel.

The rest of the herd murmured to one another in surprise and confusion. A few stamped their hooves restlessly, as if uncomfortable, while others eyed Kassel with obvious contempt.

Kassel silently walked up to the black horse, her head lowered in a gesture of submission. Without looking up, she said, 'Zelvia, I'm back and I hope—'

'Did your new master ask you to give me a message?' The strong black horse had finally opened his mouth, his tone cold and mocking. A few of the other horses laughed cruelly.

'No. Please don't say that . . . I—'

Zelvia interrupted a second time. 'How come Otis didn't come with you?'

'He's . . . he's dead. The humans killed him.' Kassel hung her head.

'You didn't die with him?' a different brown-ish-red horse behind Zelvia drawled, squinting at Kassel. The horse had long, thin legs, a well-toned body, and a proud air. 'You chose enslavement instead?'

'Darcy's right. It would've been better if you'd died too.' Zelvia stared at Kassel, his eyes filled with disgust.

'Please let me explain—'

'Explain how you became a slave to humans?' Darcy cut her off, sneering.

'I was knocked over. The humans on horseback caught up, captured me and tied me up against my will. I only escaped today. Those are the facts!' Kassel said.

'Listen to this! Humans on horseback caught up with you?' Darcy drawled, amusement in his voice. A few of the horses around him snickered. 'The idea that a wild horse could unwillingly be captured by humans riding enslaved beasts is preposterous. You must have surrendered. You're a disgrace to wild horses.'

Dilah and Ankel exchanged a glance, nodded in silent agreement, and hurried down from the ridge where they'd been watching. Zelvia's eyes shifted as he noticed the unusual pair of friends and the other horses followed his gaze. A few of the horses sniggered as the bedraggled white fox and dusty weasel sat down on either side of Kessel.

'Are these your reinforcements, traitor?' taunted Zelvia.

'They are my friends, Dilah and Ankel,' Kassel said.

'Friends? Wild horses have no friends but their own kind!'

Kassel tossed her mane – with Dilah and Ankel at her side, she seemed to have regained a little of her spirit. 'They're the ones who saved me. In my time of need, my fellow horses were nowhere to be seen. Only this fox and weasel came to my rescue. They're my saviours.'

'Hmph! When that fox hangs you out to dry, you'll be singing a different tune,' Darcy scoffed.

The way things were unfolding, it seemed Kassel's hope of returning to her herd was about to be dashed to pieces, Dilah thought. He stepped forward.

'Please allow me to say a few words, honourable leader of the horse clan,' Dilah said, lowering his head to Zelvia. 'At the risk of sounding presumptuous, I'd like to help Kassel explain.'

'Oh? Would you be so kind as to enlighten us, then?' Zelvia mimicked Dilah's formal tone, raising his eyebrows. Some of the other horses tittered.

Dilah held his head high, even though he felt as tiny as a mouse. His waist wasn't even as wide as one of Zelvia's thighs.

'As far as I can tell, it's not Kassel's fault that humans captured her. She had no choice in the matter. She doesn't like humans, much less being their slave – she certainly didn't surrender. We ran into her when we were passing by. She was so sad it just about broke our hearts. All she wants is to return to her herd. We helped cut her loose and followed her here. That's the whole story,' Dilah explained.

Zelvia was silent for a moment, then slowly asked, 'Kassel, is what the fox said true?'

Kassel nodded.

'All right then. I'm not an unreasonable leader – I believe that you were not captured willingly. But you must still prove your innocence of the greatest crime of all. Do you understand what I'm saying?' Zelvia asked matter-of-factly. Kassel nodded reluctantly.

'Lift up your foot – now!'

Kassel slowly raised up her foot, exposing the U-shaped horseshoe to her herd.

The horses gasped in surprise and horror – the nearest to Kassel even took a few steps backwards, as though afraid the shoe might burn them. Zelvia stood still, his face unchanged, his eyes narrowed. Kassel dropped her hoof to the ground.

'See, I was right,' Darcy gloated.

'How do you explain this?' Zelvia demanded.

'I . . .' Kassel hung her head in shame.

'I think it's quite clear. Kassel obviously surrendered to humans. Her master gave her the mark of a slave,' Darcy said, triumphantly. 'You know Zelvia's rules.'

'I had no choice. They forced the shoes on me!'

'Go. Don't sully my domain. You may never return,' Zelvia coldly declared.

'This is my home. Please!' Kassel begged.

'Go!' Zelvia roared, the veins in his neck bulging.

'Wait! You can't do this!' Dilah protested.

'It's none of your business, little fox! If you keep at it, don't blame me if you get a hoof in the face!' Zelvia warned.

'Dilah, Ankel, we should go. I don't want you to get hurt,' Kassel said hopelessly.

'You horses!' Ankel shouted, raising his bushy tail. 'Where were you when the humans were after Kassel? You ran for your lives, and no one stopped to help her! You abandoned one of your own. Now that she's taken the trouble to come back, you're driving her away again. She's done nothing wrong! What's wrong is your prejudice, your fear of humans and your own cowardice!'

'How dare you!' Zelvia bellowed, his eyes flashing. He reared up on his hind legs, violently shook his mane and tail, and charged towards Ankel. Dilah reacted quickly, pushing his friend out of the way before the horse's hooves came crashing down. Zelvia's front hooves left two deep holes in the ground where

Ankel had been standing.

Kassel jumped between her friends and Zelvia, shielding them with her body.

'*We're* afraid of humans?' Zelvia said. 'Humans would never dare to confront a wild horse with their bare hands, never! Instead, they use despicable means to sneak up on us – those filthy, arrogant, self-righteous humans!' The blood vessels in his eyes burnt a violent red. 'Kassel is the one who allowed herself to be enslaved. She is no longer a wild horse: she is *domesticated.*' He spat out the word as if it was a curse. But the weasel drew himself up tall, unafraid even after Zelvia's violent attack. Dilah felt his heart fill with pride in his friend.

'Domesticated horses are part of your clan, really!' Ankel argued. 'They're no different from you but for the shoes on their hooves.'

'No! That could not be further from the truth. In order to avoid predators, in order to live comfortably, in order to please their human masters, domesticated horses have sullied their own souls. They may look like us, but they're destined from birth to become slaves to humans; working hard all their life, carrying people and goods, remaining loyal and devoted, and what does that get them in the end? When they grow old and can no longer run, they are killed by their own masters!' Zelvia said. Whinnies of agreement broke out among the horses. His words had struck a chord. 'Whether she admits it or not, her shoes show that Kassel is one of *them* now, and she must leave.'

Ankel shook his head. He seemed totally determined to get through to Zelvia. He placed his small hand in front of his mouth and nibbled on his claw.

Then he grew suddenly still, his ears pricked. Dilah thought he looked as if he'd had an idea. 'So, um, you think that domesticated horses can't hold a candle to wild horses?'

'Of course!' Zelvia huffed. 'We're the fastest animals in the world!'

'Since you think so, let's have a race between you horses of noble ancestry and the "domesticated" horse who has shoes nailed to her hooves,' Ankel suggested. Dilah and Kassel stared at the weasel in astonishment. Had Ankel lost his mind?

'You don't get to make the rules! I've had enough. Get out of here!' Zelvia snorted.

'Are you scared?' Ankel goaded him.

Zelvia's eyes burnt. 'Fine. A race it is.' He faced Kassel. 'If you win the race, you may return to our herd and your friends may leave safely, but if you lose . . .'

'If I lose, I'll leave and never come back,' Kassel finished.

'*You* may leave, but *they* must pay the price for what they've said!' Zelvia glared at Dilah and Ankel as though he wanted to rip them to shreds. Dilah's heart was racing, adrenaline running through his body. If Kassel lost, he and Ankel were as good as dead. He glanced across at the weasel. Ankel looked as cool as a cucumber. 'Do you agree?' Zelvia asked.

'Of course,' Ankel agreed before Dilah or Kassel could say anything, 'that sounds fair. I have just one requirement: the race must take place on that mountain over there – let's make things a little harder, to reflect each horse's true running ability.'

Dilah and Kassel gaped at him. Kassel was a young horse – how could she compete with the strong, muscular adults, especially on difficult terrain?

'Fine – it's your funeral. Then it's all agreed,' Zelvia said, laughing unpleasantly. 'Darcy, come here. You're the fastest of our clan. Let's show these numbskulls just how fast we wild horses can run.'

Darcy puffed out his chest and stepped forward.

'It's not a fair race! Kassel is just a child, she's no match for Darcy,' the older brownish-red horse said. Several horses behind him agreed.

'Enough!' Zelvia barked, and led the herd, Dilah and Ankel towards the mountainside.

The terrain was steep and the ground was hard, strewn with sharp stones of various sizes. Dilah didn't think this kind of land was suitable for a race and wondered why Ankel had chosen it. Kassel didn't seem confident at all and hung her head the whole way to the starting point. Darcy was on cloud nine, prancing and smirking as if he'd already won.

'Viggo, you're in charge,' Zelvia said. 'We'll follow the traditional rules.'

'Your wish is my command,' an old, gravelly voice replied.

An ancient grey, all skin and bones, emerged from the crowd. He looked like a walking skeleton. He was tall, with swollen eyes. His legs, which couldn't have possibly been any thinner, wobbled as they struggled to hold up his body.

'Following the rules that have been – ahem – that have been passed down among wild horses for many years – ahem – this race will take place in a manner that is friendly and fair,' Viggo said, pausing from time to time to cough, 'and honest, in the spirit of friendship towards these animals who've come from afar –' he lowered his head to look at Dilah and Ankel, then smiled and nodded – 'and this pursuit of true strength, which we shall witness with our very eyes . . .'

Viggo droned on and on. The other horses were no longer paying attention and had begun whispering to one another.

'If my memory serves me, the last time I presided over one of these things was three years ago – ahem – it's still fresh in my mind . . . At that time, both sides were—'

'Let's dispense with the formalities and start the race!' Zelvia said impatiently.

'All right,' Viggo reluctantly agreed. 'The two competitors are – uh . . . let me see . . . Darcy!' Darcy bowed like a gentleman. The wild horses cheered and stamped their hooves. 'And Kassel!' There was only a trickle of support among the horses.

Dilah called out, 'You can do it!' and Ankel furiously clapped his paws.

'The starting point of the race is, well, it's right here. Both competitors must run to – ahem – that dead tree in the distance, then turn around and run back. The first one back here is the winner.'

Darcy and Kassel lined up, facing the dead tree in the distance. Darcy sarcastically wished Kassel good luck. The tension in Kassel's heart was written all over her face. She glanced back at Ankel and Dilah, clearly terrified for their safety should she lose. Ankel crept over to Kassel and whispered something in her ear. Kassel looked down and listened attentively, then nodded.

'Ready, set . . . go!' Viggo shouted in his squeaky old voice.

Kassel and Darcy took off, galloping as fast as they could on the bumpy terrain, manes and tails whipping behind them, hooves kicking up dust and thundering against the hard dirt. Dilah and Ankel stood in front of the watching horses, trying to make out Kassel and Darcy amid the dust. Darcy seemed relaxed. Kassel trailed a few paces behind and though she fought to keep up, the gap between them was widening slowly.

A rare smile crossed Zelvia's lips as Darcy pulled further ahead. Some of the horses cheered. Dilah paced back and forth, squinting anxiously into the dust cloud. He glanced over at Ankel, who sat on the ground, an expression of concentration and confidence on his face.

Darcy seemed dissatisfied with his lead and

picked up the pace another notch. His long, slender limbs appeared to fly over the earth, kicking up gravel in all directions. Dilah watched Kassel closely: the younger horse had noticed Darcy speeding up and was straining to catch up, sweat foaming on her coat, but the gap between them continued to increase.

A number of the wild horses stopped watching at this point: Darcy was so far in front they assumed he would win. The race had lost its suspense. But Ankel still sat there, riveted. So Dilah kept watching, trusting in his friend.

A few moments later, Dilah noticed that Darcy was slowing down. Had he run out of steam? No . . . on closer inspection, squinting into the distance, Dilah realized that Darcy's hooves seemed to have trouble handling the jagged rocks on the ground.

Though Darcy tried to hide it, his pace grew hesitant as he tried to pick the smoothest route towards the tree. Kassel, however, maintained her original speed, showing no sign of discomfort. The gap between them started to shrink rapidly. Dilah yelped with joy and excitement.

The smile had vanished from Zelvia's face. What had happened?

A few paces away from the dead tree, Kassel caught up to Darcy. The wild horses burst into an uproar.

'Woohoo – awesome!' Dilah yelled. A few of the horses cheered.

Kassel reached the dead tree, turned gracefully and galloped back toward the watching horses, tossing her head jubilantly. Darcy was clearly flustered and struggling but he kept his head down. The tide had thoroughly turned. Darcy trailed further and further behind as Kassel raced to the finishing line – as she reached it, the horses erupted in excitement. Dilah yapped excitedly, jumping up to congratulate his friend.

Darcy crossed the finishing line moments afterwards, limping slightly, the arrogant smile on his face replaced by shame.

The crowd of horses went wild as Viggo officially announced Kassel as the winner. They stamped their hooves in appreciation, the earth shaking from the rumble. Even those who had laughed at Kassel minutes ago gazed on her with new respect. Dilah sensed this would start to change how the herd felt about domesticated beasts.

Zelvia stood grim-faced and silent, watching his failed champion, his eyes burning.

'You've embarrassed me, you worthless piece of trash!' he hissed. Darcy hung his head.

'According to the terms agreed upon before the race, Kassel is allowed to return to your tribe without any conditions, and we can go,' Ankel said to Zelvia.

'Of course . . .' Zelvia said grudgingly, and Dilah could tell that every word felt like pulling teeth. 'I never go back on my promises.'

CHAPTER 7

A Time of Crisis

'Words can't express how grateful I am to you, my friends!' Kassel said to Dilah and Ankel as they drew away from the crowd to say their farewells. The sun was low in the sky, its blue deepening to violet. 'You've shown me and my entire herd how wrong we were about horseshoes. How can I ever thank you?'

'You don't need to thank us,' Dilah said, smiling. 'Knowing that you can stay with your herd is enough.'

'I'll walk with you for a bit, to see you off,' Kassel suggested.

The three young friends walked southwards across the Kvik Valley, surrounded by rocky hills. The desert turned from gold to red, a fiery glow lighting the horizon. A few crows perched on dead branches, swathed in evening sunlight, their drawn-out caws echoing across the valley.

'Ankel, I still can't figure it out – how did Darcy end up losing to me?' Kassel asked.

'It's not that Darcy did poorly – any of the wild horses would've had the same problem,' Ankel said, grinning.

Dilah frowned. 'But Kassel *is* a wild horse.'

'True, but she's different from the others,' Ankel said. 'Well, she is now.'

'Different?' Kassel asked.

Dilah suddenly understood. 'Of course!'

Kassel still looked blank.

'You're still the same as them. You just happened to benefit from human wisdom,' Ankel said.

'The horseshoes?' Kassel asked, her eyes widening.

'Yup. Zelvia despises humans, but you have to admit they know quite a lot.'

Kassel shook her head. 'I still don't understand, Ankel.'

'Humans don't put horseshoes on their horses to mark them as slaves, but to protect hooves from sharp stones and rough terrain, so that horses can run safely even on this rocky ground. Your horseshoes shouldn't be a sign of shame: you might not have wanted them, but they're a powerful tool,' Ankel said, smiling at Kassel kindly.

'Is that why you suggested the race should happen on the mountain?' Dilah asked, full of admiration for his clever friend.

Ankel nodded. 'Kassel had no chance of winning a short-distance race held on level ground, but on difficult terrain, she had an advantage.'

Kassel blinked. 'I remember what you whispered to me before the race . . .'

'I told you to keep running no matter what, even if you were losing. I was worried you'd lose heart after falling behind at the beginning.'

'Did you see the look on Zelvia's face after you won, Kassel?' Dilah said, laughing.

'Priceless!' Kassel snorted.

The three laughed and joked as they walked through the dusk, so it was only when they briefly fell silent that Dilah's ears suddenly pricked up. He hadn't been concentrating before, but now he could hear faint sounds echoing through the rocky outcrops on their left. The sounds quickly grew closer. He heard the scratch of multiple footsteps padding over the ground, and soft panting. He whirled around, and froze in fear as he realized who was emerging from the long shadows nearby.

A dozen or so blue foxes, headed by a lean white fox with deep-set, bloodshot eyes, his hind leg dragging. *Carl.* The pack was travel-worn and dusty but their eyes gleamed as they ran towards Dilah, whose paws felt as if they were glued to the sun-warmed ground. Carl's eyes narrowed as they fixed on him.

Ankel and Kassel turned to their friend questioningly. 'Is that—' Ankel started.

'Yes. That's Carl,' Dilah said, his voice weak with fear. He'd thought Carl and the blue foxes had lost his trail, assuming him dead and the moonstone lost.

'We finally found you,' Carl beamed, his sharp teeth catching the dying sunlight. 'Long time no see, Dilah. You've grown.'

'H-how did you know I was still alive?' Dilah asked, his voice trembling, glad of Ankel and Kassel standing close on either side.

'When we didn't find your body under the cliff, I ordered my foxes to search for the moonstone along the beach. Eventually, we picked up your tracks. We lost you a few times, but at last . . .' He gazed hungrily at the moonstone package around Dilah's neck.

Dilah backed away slightly, his fur bristling.

'I'm sure you can guess why I've come, but this time it's different . . .' Carl paused, his face serious. 'I want us to work together.'

'What?' Dilah hadn't expected this.

'Yes. I need your help.' Carl limped closer to Dilah. 'You know how to use the moonstone, don't you?'

'I don't know what you mean,' Dilah coldly replied.

'Don't try to fool me,' Carl growled. 'I've noticed your direction – it's straight and true. You know where you're heading, which means something is guiding you. I'm certain you've figured out how to use the moonstone to find Ulla's secret treasure.'

Dilah was silent.

Carl softened his voice. 'That's why we need to work together. If I were to steal the moonstone from you, I'd waste time figuring out how to use it. It'd be better—'

'It'd be better to make Dilah go with you to find the treasure, and then get rid of him at the earliest opportunity, so that you could have the treasure all to yourself?' Ankel finished for him, drawing himself up tall.

'Who are you?' Carl scowled. 'And this one too?' He gazed up at Kassel, snarling.

'It's none of your business who we are,' Ankel said, his voice full of disdain. Kassel tossed her head dismissively.

'Did Dilah make a couple of friends?'

Carl looked at Ankel with contempt, then continued, returning his attention to Dilah. 'Whatever. You're a smart fox. You've come a long way on your own, but you can imagine the difficulties and obstacles you'll face on the rest of your journey. You can't find Ulla's treasure alone – or with these two creatures. But if us foxes work together, I know we can make it. What do you say?'

'What about Jens?' Dilah asked, realizing the patriarch of the foxes was missing from the pack.

'He's gone.' Carl spoke slowly and deliberately, his expression unreadable. 'Tragically killed by an avalanche.'

Despite the sun's waning heat, Dilah felt cold to his core.

'I'm the new patriarch, Dilah. You might say that helping me is your duty as an Arctic fox.' He swished his tail. 'So, what's your answer?'

Dilah didn't have to think twice. 'No, never! I'd never work with you,' he said firmly.

'You're sure you won't regret it?'

'Of course I won't regret it!' Dilah said

bluntly. 'You would have killed me for the moonstone before. How can I possibly trust you now?'

'Then it seems that our negotiations have failed . . .' Carl barked out a command and the blue foxes began closing in on Dilah and his friends.

'So this is how you foxes like to solve problems,' Ankel said.

'Let's start with this pesky weasel,' Carl said, narrowing his eyes at Ankel. 'Although he's little more than a snack . . .'

'Then throw me in as the main course, and you'll have plenty to fill everyone up!' Kassel stepped forwards, shielding Ankel. 'If you can catch me, that is.'

Carl looked up and stared icily at Kassel, as though he'd just noticed her.

'This is none of your business, wild horse. Get out of the way!' Carl snarled.

'And if I won't?'

'Dilah's a fugitive from our fox clan. I'm taking him back now. Stay out of our fox affairs!' Carl warned, his sharp teeth bared.

Despite his lame leg, the white fox was strong and muscular – and he had twelve blue warriors at his back. Dilah knew Kassel couldn't withstand them all. He hated the thought of his friends getting hurt.

'Take Ankel away, Kassel. Let me handle this,' Dilah said, his voice low and persuasive. 'Please.'

But the horse shook her head. 'No. I will never abandon a friend in a time of need!' Kassel proudly declared. She turned to face Carl. 'I don't care if he's a fugitive – I won't let you have Dilah.'

'As you wish . . .' Carl barked a second command.

In the blink of an eye, several Arctic foxes pounced on the horse, digging their sharp claws into her back. She reared up, the whites of her eyes rolling. A few foxes lost their grip, tumbling to the ground and leaving streaks of blood on Kassel's white coat.

'Ankel, hide!' Dilah shouted desperately – he knew the weasel couldn't survive a fox attack. Ankel retreated quickly behind a nearby rock, hiding in the deepening shadow.

The rest of the foxes charged at Kassel's legs, her tail, her neck. Kassel bucked, desperately trying to shake the foxes off her body – but there were too many. Dilah rushed over to help, but he was knocked down, slamming hard into a rock. His head felt heavy, the world around him spun. As he regained focus, he realized Carl was standing over him, viciously staring him down, his sharp claws pinning him to the ground. In the sky above them, the moon was rising and stars began to dot the velvet sky.

'Tell me the secret of the moonstone!' Carl growled.

'Never!'

Dilah clenched his teeth and kicked upwards with all his might, his paws connecting with the patriarch's belly. Carl was caught off guard and fell backwards on to the sandy earth, sand ballooning around him in a cloud. Dilah started to run over to Kassel but Carl recovered quickly, lunging at him a second time and easily overpowering the younger fox. Dilah's head hit the ground once more, his ears ringing. Carl nipped at the seaweed cord around his neck, tearing the moonstone from his chest and dangling it over his face. Dilah tried his best to try to break free but Carl was too strong.

'You're still a far cry from your father,' Carl said, gazing down at the smaller fox.

Dilah's eyes widened. 'What do you mean?' he said.

Nearby, Kassel neighed fiercely and Carl's attention was drawn away. The horse's two front hooves flew up as she kicked out with extraordinary power, flinging an entire clutch of foxes off her body. The Arctic foxes retreated, slinking into the shadows. Kassel was fuming, the veins on her forehead bulging, her nostrils flaring and sweat foaming alongside the blood on her coat. Now, she had the upper hand. Her front hooves stomped down on a vixen rushing toward her. Kassel bucked her back hooves, and a second fox was knocked into the air, landing several paces away, and staying motionless on the ground. The other foxes circled Kassel warily now, bristling with nerves.

'Attack!' Carl demanded of his remaining foxes, his attention drawn away from the small fox under his paws.

Dilah took the opportunity: he snatched the moonstone back from Carl's jaws, holding the package firmly in his mouth. Carl's attention snapped towards him and he growled, low and deep.

Hooves pounded the earth nearby: Kassel was charging at breakneck speed, right towards Carl and Dilah. The patriarch leapt out of her path, releasing Dilah, who scrambled to his feet, the moonstone safe in his mouth. Kassel skidded to a halt, her hooves furiously scratching the ground, kicking up plumes of dust. A safe distance away, Carl seethed with rage, his chest heaving violently.

'Attack her!' he barked again, but when the remaining blue foxes hesitated again, Kassel rushed forwards aggressively. The Arctic foxes scattered in panic. Despite the blood streaking her white coat, Kassel was stronger and there was nothing Carl could do about it.

'Today's your lucky day,' Carl hissed at Dilah, 'but we'll meet again, Dilah – and if your big friend isn't around, you'd better be afraid.' He turned away and slunk into the dark-red remains of the dusk, his blue pack following at his heels.

Ankel peeked out from behind his rock,

joining Dilah and Kassel when he saw the foxes had left.

'Are you all right?' Kassel asked the two smaller animals.

'That's what we should be asking you,' Ankel said. 'You're covered in blood.'

But Kassel tossed her head dismissively. 'Pah! Just scratches. When I was a young foal and my mother taught me to run, I often fell and ended up hurt much worse than this.'

'Kassel,' Dilah started, 'without your help today, we wouldn't have . . .'

'Consider it a thank you.'

'Carl and the foxes are still nearby. We need to lose them,' Dilah said. 'And you need to get back to your herd and recover. Let's say goodbye.'

But Kassel shook her head. 'Before we do, I have an idea to help you ditch the foxes as quickly as possible . . .'

'Woohoo – this is so cool!' Ankel shrieked. He rode on Kassel's back as the horse barrelled along, his small paws clutching her mane, his whole body whipping in the wind. 'I'm flying!'

Dilah laughed as he too held on tight. Kassel galloped through the yellow valley. At full speed, no longer checking her pace so Dilah and Ankel could keep up, she was impossibly fast. Behind them, the huge red moon rose higher and higher. Dilah yapped loudly, enjoying the thrill of the speed.

The night deepened, hours passed and the stars glimmered overhead. The quiet of the valley was broken only by the caws of the crows and the beating of Kassel's hooves. Kassel's white coat shone silver in the moonlight. The horse knew the valley like the back of her hoof and weaved through the hidden shortcuts that ran through the rocky land. The motion of Kassel's run soothed Dilah until he shut his eyes . . .

Dilah jerked awake: he realized he'd been dozing for quite some time, somehow still clinging tightly to Kassel's back. Ankel was asleep at his side. The sun was rising now, and its golden light shone on a vast wasteland;

barren and cracked earth spreading into the distance. Low scraggly weeds were the only living things in sight. Kassel slowed down to a trot. She was growing tired at last. The Kvik Valley was far behind them, reduced to a series of small yellow slopes on the horizon. They'd left Carl and his pack a long way back.

Kassel stopped and Dilah leapt to the ground. The horse gently shook her shoulders to dislodge her second passenger. Ankel fell off, landing on his bum.

'Ow! What? Where are we?' the weasel asked groggily.

'I've carried you out of the valley, as far as I could go,' Kassel replied, her voice rough with exhaustion. 'Now you're on your own. Since those foxes chased you all the way from the Arctic, they're bound to keep following you. Be careful.'

'Thank you, Kassel,' Dilah said, smiling up at her. 'I didn't expect you to carry us so far. With this head start, we might have a chance of outrunning Carl's pack.'

'You have more than repaid any debt you

owed us,' Ankel added, rubbing the sleep from his eyes.

'Good luck, my friends. We'll meet again.' Kassel turned around and took off back towards the valley.

The sound of her hooves faded away, leaving Ankel and Dilah alone.

CHAPTER 8

The River

Dilah and Ankel walked through the barren land, guided by the moonstone, occasionally spotting lynxes and deer. These strangers never approached, but stared at the pair in surprise. It was probably hard to imagine what an Arctic fox and weasel were doing together, especially in a place like this.

Eventually, the barren land gave way to low wheat fields, a city rising beyond. Even from a distance they could see the city was bustling with activity, and a pungent smell – humans, waste and petrol – wafted from its direction. Huge chimneys spewed black smoke into the sky. From afar, the entire city was cloaked in a grey haze.

Dilah and Ankel hadn't been able to find anything to drink for some time. They were parched, tongues sticking to the roofs of their mouths – even the strawberries they found on the city outskirts were pitifully shrivelled up. Now it was late in the day, the sun was setting and the friends were desperate for water.

'I swear that as soon as we see a stream, the first thing I'm going to do is stick my head in!' Ankel said.

The dry wind blew in Dilah's face, rustling the green plants surrounding them both. 'Hang on . . . there are more plants here than there were before we reached the city, which—' Dilah began.

'There's water nearby!' Ankel excitedly burst out, his eyes bright. 'Let's go!'

They followed the green strip, skirting the city until, at last, they reached a river emerging from its southern edge. Tall weeds grew askew on either bank, and the dark-green water flowed slowly, gurgling, a string of bubbles floating on the surface. Ankel cheered and rushed over, plunging his head into the water and desperately lapping it up.

'Hey, wait!' Dilah warned, catching a whiff of something foul. A dead fish floated in the current.

But it was too late.

'Ah – so refreshing . . . don't you want some?' Ankel asked, emerging at last and sticking out his full round belly.

'Ankel, you shouldn't have drunk that water!'

'It did taste a bit strange . . .' Ankel said, smacking his lips. 'But it's better than dying of thirst!'

They carried on, following the river south as the sun sank. Dilah forced himself not to drink the water, however thirsty he felt – and soon, his caution was justified. Ankel started to slow down, his breath laboured.

'Are you OK?' Dilah asked.

'My stomach aches,' Ankel said. 'I feel like

I'm going to throw up.'

A few paces on, Ankel curled up on the ground, moaning and unable to continue. Dilah watched in alarm, feeling totally helpless. An indescribable fear spread through his body. Ankel's life could be in danger and he had no idea how to help him.

A few vultures circled above and Dilah yapped at them angrily. He wasn't ready to give up on his friend! He'd made a promise to Azalea to keep Ankel safe. He picked him up gently by the scruff of his neck, as his own mother had lifted him as a child. He had to find help. A hill sloped up from the banks of the river – perhaps he'd be able to spot something from higher up.

'Dilah, I'm scared,' Ankel squeaked feebly as a light breeze blew through the white fox's fur.

The grass on the hill was thicker, a sleek glossy green in the fading sunlight, like a freshly painted picture that hadn't yet dried.

'I'm sorry that I couldn't help you find the treasure. Mum was right – I should have stayed behind.' Ankel's eyes were filled with despair. His breathing was becoming weaker and weaker. Dilah placed him carefully on the top of the hill.

'No, don't talk like this. You'll be fine.' But Dilah's voice quivered, his eyes welling up with tears.

Something scampered through the grass nearby. Dilah glanced up, but before he could figure out what it was, a fluffy grey puffball flew out of the undergrowth and thwacked him in the side. He staggered, shook out his fur, and stared at his attacker.

A large grey rabbit was staring right back, every bit as shocked. The rabbit had big buck teeth poking out of from his chubby face, a mouth speckled with small black dots, and drooping ears, nicked in several places. Dilah blinked at him in astonishment.

'What's wrong with him?' The grey rabbit said, noticing Ankel.

'He's sick,' Dilah said. 'He drank the river water.'

The grey rabbit hopped over to Ankel, bent

down, and inspected him carefully. He gently lifted one of Ankel's eyelids, then leant over his chest, listening to the weasel's heartbeat with his long, battered ears, his eyes narrowing.

The rabbit looked like he knew what he was doing, and Dilah couldn't help the way his own heart rose in hope. 'Can you save him? Will he get better?'

'I'm not sure, but I'll try . . .' the grey rabbit said.

He circled around Ankel, who was limp and unconscious on the grass. He bent over him, lost in thought, muttering something to himself.

'Rabbit ear grass!' he burst out at last, straightening up.

'Rabbit ear grass?' Dilah repeated.

'You carry him. Come with me, hurry!' The rabbit spun around and jumped back into the glossy green grass, quickly bounding toward the other side of the hill.

Carrying Ankel, Dilah followed. They stopped in front of a patch of thick underbrush that was almost as tall as Dilah. The rabbit parted the dense greenery with his paws, and a crystal-clear stream slid into view, glittering like fish scales in the sun.

The grey rabbit fumbled about the under-growth. Dilah tried to stay calm as he set Ankel down by the water. The stream was so clean you could see right through it, to the colourful pebbles speckling the bed. Small fish darted in the thin currents.

Dilah walked over to the rabbit and saw that he was tugging on a plant. The entire plant had only one green stalk, wrapped in layers of thick green leaves. There was a cluster of small blue flowers on top, emitting a strange, sweet-smelling scent. To Dilah's amazement, the leaves, both big and small, looked like rabbit's ears. Rabbit ear grass!

'Can this cure him?' Dilah asked eagerly.

'I'm not sure, but this is the only thing I can think of to try.' The rabbit crammed the whole plant into his mouth, his cheeks puffing up. He chewed and chewed, then hurried to Ankel's side.

Dilah lifted up the little weasel, and helped

him to open his mouth. The rabbit spat the chewed-up grass into his paw, and stuffed it in. Ankel's throat was blocked. He gulped instinctively, swallowing all of the medicine.

'Is he going to be all right?' Dilah whispered a moment later.

The grey rabbit let out a long sigh. 'The truth is, I don't know. All we can do now is wait.'

Dilah looked at the rabbit. 'What's your name?'

'Little Bean.'

'Thank you, Little Bean. You've done what you can.' Dilah glanced back at Ankel, lying on the soft grass. 'Why did the water poison him?'

'Humans have polluted the river. You can't drink from it any more. Many animals around here have died from drinking it.'

'What about this stream?' Dilah asked. He felt faint with thirst.

'Of course. This is the water source for our rabbit clan – it's sweet and delicious!' Little Bean proudly declared.

Dilah rushed over to the stream and gulped several mouthfuls. The pure water was the best thing he had ever tasted – he felt reborn. When he was finished, he sat at Ankel's side, watching his little friend breathing. Was it his imagination, or was the weasel resting a little easier now?

Little Bean had hopped into the thick undergrowth, where he sat by himself on a pile of yellow weeds, gazing at his big feet, his ears drooping.

'Is something bothering you?' Dilah asked, walking over to him.

Little Bean gently shook his head.

'When you bumped into me earlier, you were in a hurry. Was it something important?'

'I was rushing to attend the ceremony for our patron saint. But it's too late now,' Little Bean said.

'Patron saint?' Dilah asked curiously – did rabbits have their own patron saint too?

'M-hmm. The Jade Hare, Buona.' Little Bean gazed up at the moon. 'Today is the fullest and brightest moon of the year. Our tribe will hold a grand ceremony to pay tribute to her.'

'What will happen now that you've missed it?'

'I might be scolded by the elders, forced to do chores, or have to fast for a day . . .'

'But it's not your fault! You had to help us, or my friend would have died. Why don't you explain?'

Little Bean shook his head. 'Whenever there are more than three rabbits around, I get too nervous to speak. I'm really rather useless.'

'Isn't there someone who could help you?' Dilah asked.

'I don't have any friends. No one wants to be my friend,' Little Bean said bluntly.

'Why?' Dilah couldn't believe it.

'Look at me! I'm ugly. Everyone avoids me.'

Dilah was outraged. 'You're not ugly! And anyway, you're so kind-hearted! You saved my friend's life without thinking twice. That makes you the most beautiful rabbit in the world!'

'Thank you. Really, thank you.' Little Bean's eyes were moist. 'If only others thought so.'

A moaning noise interrupted them. *Ankel!* Dilah rushed to his friend's side, Little Bean close at his heels.

'Dilah . . . ?' Ankel's eyes gently fluttered open.

'You're awake!' Dilah shouted, the weight on his heart lifting.

'It worked!' Little Bean clapped his paws in delight. 'He'll be fine. He just needs to sleep it off.'

'What happened?' said Ankel, blinking blearily at the rabbit. 'Who's this?'

'This is Little Bean,' Dilah said. 'He saved your life, Ankel.'

Little Bean smiled bashfully. Together, he and Dilah helped Ankel to the stream where he

drank the clean, fresh water, then lay back and shut his eyes.

'Now that your friend's all right, Dilah, I should probably be heading back,' the rabbit mumbled, the smile on his face fading.

'Take us with you. Maybe we can help explain,' Dilah said, already nudging Ankel to his feet. 'Ankel, come on. If we don't help Little Bean, he might be punished.'

'Uuurgh,' Ankel replied groggily.

'Thanks,' said Little Bean, 'but you don't need—'

'Take us!' Dilah insisted.

Little Bean nodded in agreement, his big round eyes fixed on Dilah, then silently turned to leave. Carrying the semi-conscious Ankel on his back, Dilah followed.

CHAPTER 9

The Trial

After a while, Little Bean stopped. He sat up on his hind legs and peered out of the weeds and scrubland towards a gigantic tree nearby. Dilah followed his gaze. Ankel was draped across the fox's back, clinging feebly to his fur. The tree stood all alone, towering over the flat meadow like a humongous mushroom. It looked ancient, with a thick trunk and lush, leafy branches, tangles of vines drooping from the dense greenery. A ginormous carrot hung from one of the vines. The ground beneath the glossy green tree buzzed with activity. Sitting together in circles were hundreds of rabbits – big and small, tall and short, black and white, brown and grey.

Then, a giant yellow rabbit waddled out from behind the trunk. Dilah blinked. Were his eyes playing tricks on him? He'd never seen or heard of such a large rabbit! It was even taller than Kassel, with a roly-poly, fluffy body. The rest of the rabbits seemed tiny by comparison.

The other rabbits made room for the giant rabbit as he wobbled towards the swaying

carrot. There was a moment of silence as everyone gazed reverently at it. The giant rabbit raised his paws and chanted something to the carrot in hushed tones.

Then the giant rabbit stood up – his head almost brushing against the lower branches of the tall tree – and shouted at the full moon: 'Oh great and holy Buona – beneath this sacred tree, I offer unto you the biggest carrot from this year's harvest in thanks for your blessings.'

The giant rabbit's voice rang out over the thick grass, as loud and clear as a bell. Dilah glanced at Little Bean and discovered he was clasping his paws and praying under his breath.

'You don't want to go over?' Dilah whispered.

But Little Bean shook his head. 'The ceremony's already started, I can't interrupt it now. We'll wait till it's done.'

Tick tick, tick tick . . . A rhythmic clicking started up from beneath the big tree. Five rabbits sat neatly in a row, holding a pebble in each paw and striking them together in unison. The giant rabbit sat across from the pebble rabbits, waving his paws like a conductor, occasionally shouting, 'One-two, one-two,' to keep the rhythm. But after a while, the giant rabbit's voice trailed off, and his movements slowed and stopped, his head comically slumping into the thick fur on his chest. He nodded off, his snores rumbling like thunder. A rabbit next to him nudged him. The giant rabbit raised his head at once and waved his paws haphazardly, trying to find his place.

The rabbits formed several rings around the tree, waving their paws to the beat, wiggling their bottoms from side to side. Their movements were so perfectly in sync that Dilah was sure they must've performed this dance more than a hundred times. A few minutes later, the rabbits began to change their movements. They circled the tree, waving their paws and chanting 'Buona, Buona, Buona'.

'This is the bunny hop, an essential part of the end of the ceremony,' Little Bean explained under his breath.

The dance lasted for ages. Dilah settled down in the grass, his tail flicking as he watched, while Ankel snoozed intermittently at his side. Little Bean ghosted the dance's movements. The moon's light draped a silvery cloak over the prairie and the gigantic tree. As the beating of the pebbles eventually ceased, all the rabbits returned to their original spots – the ceremony was over. The giant rabbit doddered away from the tree as best as he could. The other rabbits formed a wide path to let him through. Little Bean stirred at Dilah's side, then bounded over to the group without saying a word. Dilah followed, with Ankel once again clinging onto his back.

'Lord Lund – wait!' Little Bean called.

'Huh?' The giant rabbit slowly turned, the other rabbits following his lead. Little Bean stumbled and fell down, but quickly pulled himself back up and kept on running.

'L-Lord Lund, I-I . . .' Little Bean huffed and puffed, catching up with the giant rabbit and his followers.

The smaller rabbits fell quiet, fixing Dilah, Ankel and Little Bean with cold, stony glares.

'You're late, my dear child,' Lund said

gently, bending down to peer at Little Bean with his huge eyes. The giant rabbit's fluffy yellow head was bigger than Little Bean's whole body. 'You missed the ceremony. Why?'

Little Bean's whiskers twitched in obvious discomfort as he gazed down at his paws, standing as still as stone. He appeared to be unable to speak.

'This is a once-a-year event,' Lund added slowly.

Dilah stepped forward. 'My friend was poisoned and almost died. Little Bean was absent because he was saving him,' he said, rushing to Little Bean's defence.

'Oh?' Lund turned his attention to Dilah.

'How could you bring a *fox* here?' asked an elderly grey rabbit, frowning at Little Bean in disapproval.

'I-I . . .' Little Bean was tongue-tied, wringing his paws nervously.

'Hmm. This kind of pure white fox is rare,' Lund mumbled to himself with great interest.

'Lord Lund, how should we deal with Little Bean?' the old grey rabbit asked.

'He missed the ceremony,' another rabbit piped up.

'This is extremely disrespectful towards Buona,' yet another cut in.

'A trial should be held according to the laws of the council,' an identical pair of white rabbits chimed in at the same time. These two rabbits had wide chins, long faces, and raspy, harsh voices.

'The Crystal Sisters are correct,' Lund said, nodding sagely. 'A trial, yes.'

'Lord Lund, Little Bean not only missed the ceremony, but it also sounds as if he has spread our medical secrets to outsiders,' a black, curly-haired rabbit added, hopping over to Lund's side. His voice was deep, his stern glare fixed on Dilah.

'You have a point, Bennett. Matters involving outsiders should also be carefully investigated,' Lund replied, his words long and slow. All of a sudden, his head slouched into his fur ball of a body, and he let out a long yawn.

Dilah was impatient. Why couldn't the rabbits understand? 'You're blaming him unfairly. He was rushing to the ceremony when— Lord Lund?'

A deafening snore rumbled from the great rabbit, drool pooling in the corners of his mouth.

The rabbits exchanged awkward glances. Finally, a white rabbit with a gruff face hopped forward and poked Lund in the belly. Lund snorted awake. 'What is it, Harrison?' he said to the gruff white rabbit. Then, he carried on speaking as if he'd never fallen asleep. 'White Fox, you also have a point. I watched Little Bean grow up. He has a good heart. I don't believe he'd do anything to harm our tribe. But I can't decide this on my own. What does the council think?'

Five rabbits huddled round in a small circle, murmuring in low voices. Eventually, the black curly rabbit called Bennett hopped forward.

'According to articles seven and twenty-four of council law, Little Bean must be tried in public by the highest criminal court,' Bennett announced.

'What?!' Dilah was shocked. Little Bean

quivered at his side. 'This is so stupid! Haven't you heard anything I said?'

'This is a criminal case brought against you by the council,' Bennett told Little Bean. 'Of course, you can ask your *friends* to come to your defence.'

An unkind snigger ran through the watching rabbits and Dilah remembered what Little Bean had said: he had no friends.

'But from now on,' Bennett continued, 'every word you say will be considered part of your confession.'

'Oh my,' Lund said, flustered. 'Well, if you're all determined to do this . . .'

A number of rabbits emerged from the crowd and marched Little Bean away.

'You guys should go.' Little Bean glanced back at Dilah, flashing a wavering smile. 'There's no good defence for what I've done, anyway. Goodbye, and thank you for trying!'

Dilah's heart ached as he watched Little Bean stumble into the distance.

'No way,' he muttered under his breath. Determined to save Little Bean no matter what, he quietly trailed behind, carrying Ankel on his back.

The perfectly round full moon was mounted high in the sky as they walked across the prairie. At last, they came to a large, oddly shaped dark-green hill. It looked like a huge upside-down funnel. The top of the hill narrowed into an oval-shaped tip that towered into the air. The end of the tip was open, and a warm orange light flickered inside.

The rabbits climbed the hill and disappeared inside. Upon reaching the top and peering into the hole, Dilah's eyes widened. The inside was completely hollowed out and housed a cylindrical hall, constructed from brown, compacted earth. Four staircases were symmetrically arranged around the opening, each leading down to the floor inside. A bonfire blazed and crackled in the middle of the hall. The rabbits marched Little Bean down one flight of stairs, Dilah and Ankel following behind.

When he reached the floor, which was paved with dark pebbles, Dilah realized the moon was perfectly framed in the circular opening above.

From here, it was also possible to see how the circular walls were riddled with small arched holes, like a honeycomb, eight levels in all.

Ankel stirred on Dilah's back. 'This must be the courthouse,' he whispered into Dilah's ear.

Little Bean sat quietly in the centre of the huge hall. For a moment, all was silent – but then the pitter-patter of footsteps echoed through the space. Five rabbits emerged from the largest arched hole, directly opposite Little Bean. Dilah instantly recognized them as the five rabbits who'd conferred earlier: Bennett, the black rabbit, hopped out in front and stared at Dilah with hard, unwelcoming eyes. The older grey rabbit was at his side, apparently preoccupied. The thin white rabbit, Harrison, emerged next, his face unreadable. Lastly, the white twins, the Crystal Sisters, stepped into the orange-red light, murmuring in low voices, nodding from time to time. Dilah had a sinking feeling in his stomach.

Gradually, the din in the hall grew louder and louder as new arrivals poked their heads through the arched holes in the wall, noses twitching, eyes twinkling in the firelight. The spectators whispered to each other, throwing Dilah and Ankel suspicious glances. Soon, all the rabbits had taken their places – but none of them had arrived through the central hole in the ceiling. At last, Dilah understood the function of the arches in the walls: there was obviously an extensive underground network inside the hill. The rabbits' multiple burrows and tunnels led here, where they could discuss important matters or hold trials.

'All right, it's about time,' Harrison muttered to the other four rabbits of the council, then turned around to face everyone. 'Let the trial begin!'

The hall fell silent.

The five rabbits of the council lined up in a row, perched on a high stone platform across from Little Bean. They gazed at him over the fire pit, the flickering flames sending shadows across their faces. Several rabbits guarded Little Bean on either side, and other guards kept watch over the four staircases. Dilah stood behind Little Bean with Ankel on his back.

'Council members, it's regrettable that we are here in criminal court on this day of holy ceremony, but we have no choice. Little Bean was not only absent from today's ceremony, but he is suspected of passing our medical secrets to outsiders. We must put him on trial for his crimes,' Bennett said in a low voice, scanning the various archways, pausing for a second as his dark eyes swept over Dilah. 'He must answer to the following charges: one count of sacrilege, and one count of collaborating with the enemy,' Bennett finished tersely.

'Well, Little Bean, would you like to defend yourself?' the thin white rabbit, Harrison, asked.

'I-I—'

'Or would you like to admit to your crimes?'

'N-no!' Little Bean stuttered.

'Let me defend him!' Dilah said, stepping forwards.

'Hush, Fox! You can't defend Little Bean!' Harrison declared.

'Why?'

'According to article ten of the charter of the

council court, only friends of the accused can defend the accused in the council court, and Little Bean has no friends.'

'I'm his friend,' Dilah said, staring Harrison in the eye, 'and always will be!'

The hall was suddenly in uproar. Little Bean glanced back at Dilah. His black-spotted mouth hung slightly open, his eyes filled with tears.

Harrison, too angry to speak, turned to Bennett for help.

'From a procedural standpoint, it's a reasonable request. Since the fox considers Little Bean a friend, he has the right to defend him,' Bennett said grudgingly.

'Regarding the charge of sacrilege, I begged Little Bean to treat the weasel. He didn't intend to miss the ceremony,' Dilah said. 'Ankel would have died if it weren't for his help.'

'We have already established the fact of his absence. He must be punished for violating the law, regardless of the reason or excuse,' Harrison said.

'But the second accusation isn't valid. Why should saving my friend be considered collaborating with the enemy?'

'Because foxes are natural enemies of rabbits, and the friend of an enemy is also considered an enemy. Little Bean helped the enemy, which makes him guilty of collaborating with the enemy,' Bennett icily explained.

'Wait, I have something to say,' the elderly grey rabbit said, a worried expression on his face.

'What is it, Albert?' Bennett snapped.

Albert cleared his throat. 'Little Bean may have been coerced into saving the fox's friend, whether through external pressure or having his life threatened. The charges for this kind of involuntary violation of the law should be reduced as appropriate. So, Little Bean, answer me: did the fox force you to save the weasel?'

'No,' Little Bean replied, his head bowed.

'Think carefully. If you answer "yes", things will take a favourable turn for you,' Albert said.

'No . . . no, I volunteered my help,' Little Bean asserted.

'You're too naive, Albert. If Little Bean didn't want to save the weasel, he could've given him a different herb. But, as you can see, the weasel has been saved. This is clearly a result of our medical skills,' Bennett said coldly. 'Now that the situation has been clarified, the senior judiciary committee will begin its deliberations. Council members will vote on the preliminary verdict, and if it is approved by a majority of members, the verdict will take effect. If it does not pass, the charges against Little Bean will be withdrawn immediately.'

The flames grew stronger and stronger, the air in the hall growing heavy and hot. Blue moonlight shone through the opening of the dome, spilling on to the black pebbled floor. Little Bean kept his head down, standing as still as stone. His fate was out of his paws, Dilah thought, his pulse jittering. All he could do was wait and pray that the punishment wouldn't be too harsh. The five rabbits huddled in a circle on the stone platform.

After they finished their deliberations, Bennett addressed the crowd. 'Ladies and gentleman, as the chief judge, I will deliver the criminal council court's preliminary verdict regarding the case against Little Bean.' His face was half hidden by the flickering of the fire in the middle of the hall, his black eyes glowing. His voice sounded as though it was coming from the moon, framed in the round hole above the court: loud and clear, calm, and indifferent. 'Little Bean is found guilty of sacrilege – violating article seven of the council law – and is hereby banished from the Elnis Rabbit Tribe. I also find him guilty of violating article twenty-four of the council law – collaborating with the enemy – and he is therefore sentenced to punishment by water.'

'Punishment by water?' Dilah repeated, shocked. 'What's that?'

'The animal who is to be punished is thrown in the water and abandoned,' Ankel quietly answered.

'What?!' Dilah fumed, blood rushing to his head.

'Calm down! This is just a preliminary verdict. Wait until they finish voting,' Ankel whispered.

'Council members are invited to cast their votes!' Harrison called out. 'Those in favour of the preliminary verdict, please show your eyes. Those who are opposed, please keep them closed.'

The rabbits in the archways angled their faces toward the fire, opening their eyes wide so that they reflected the flames. And then something incredible happened: the archways of those rabbits who were in favour of the verdict shone like lightbulbs, and the archways of those rabbits who were opposed were pitch-black. In this way, the votes could be easily counted. So far, as far as Dilah could tell, the majority of the rabbits had their eyes open. His heart sank further.

'I don't think it's necessary to count the votes. The preliminary verdict has been approved by an overwhelming majority of members,' Bennett said. 'Now I formally proclaim that the criminal council court's preliminary verdict against Little Bean has been approved: he is sentenced to punishment by water, to be carried out immediately!'

Two rabbits yanked Little Bean up from the ground and prepared to drag him out of the courtroom.

'Wait! You can't do this!' Dilah roared, his eyes blazing with rage. 'The trial wasn't fair – I won't let you touch a single hair on his head!' He snarled at the rabbit guards by Little Bean's side – they backed away, ears flattened with fright.

'Fox, are you sure you want to interfere in our trial?' Bennett cautioned.

Guards surrounded Dilah, Ankel and Little Bean, but Dilah remained glued to Little Bean's side. How many rabbits could he fight off, he wondered, grimly. He was stronger, but there were so many. The tension in the hall was thick enough to cut.

Then a small voice piped up from over Dilah's shoulder. 'Since Little Bean has been expelled from the rabbit tribe, your laws have no binding effect on him. As such, the crime of collaborating with the enemy is irrelevant,' Ankel said, breaking the dead silence in the hall.

A murmuring started up among the rabbits and Dilah felt his heart lift with hope.

'He has a point,' said the grey judge, Albert. 'If we've banished Little Bean, he is no longer a member of the tribe, so how can we sentence him to water punishment?' The five rabbit judges huddled together and engaged in a heated discussion.

After some time, Bennett emerged from the group, gritting his teeth. 'All right, all right. The council agrees to your proposal. Little Bean is banished.'

'He may never return!' Harrison snarled in frustration.

Dilah leapt up so enthusiastically that Ankel nearly lost grip on his fur. 'Little Bean, let's go!'

The three were permitted to spend the night under the gigantic sacred tree.

Early the next morning, Dilah was woken by Ankel tugging his tail. Dilah opened his eyes to bright sunlight and squinted at his friend.

'We have to go now, or Little Bean will be in trouble!' said Ankel.

Little Bean was sitting beneath the sacred tree, gazing up at the sky.

'Little Bean,' said Ankel, approaching the rabbit a little shyly. 'You saved my life, but I haven't even really met you yet. I'm Ankel. Thank you. You're my lifesaver!' Ankel bowed deeply.

'No, you don't need to thank me. I should be thanking you,' Little Bean said, his face turning red. 'Pleased to meet you.'

'What will you do now, Little Bean?' Dilah asked, cocking his head curiously.

The rabbit blinked. 'I don't know.'

'Of course,' Ankel started, 'you could always join us on our adventure.'

Little Bean smiled shyly. 'That sounds exciting. What kind of adventure?'

As they set off, brilliant sunlight scattered the mist that rose up from the grass. Birds chattered and flowers bloomed. They followed a small path, heading away from the rabbit tribe. As they rounded a bend at the edge of the rabbit tribe's territory, Dilah spotted Lund, Albert, and a few others he didn't recognise waiting for them. *Are they here to catch Little Bean and take him back?*

'My poor child,' Lund's loud and clear voice rang out. When he saw Little Bean, the giant rabbit lovingly opened his massive paws.

'Lord Lund!' Little Bean greeted him with excitement.

'Albert's eyes were full of tenderness as he stepped forward next, holding out his arms.

'Teacher!' Little Bean cried, his eyes damp as he embraced the old rabbit.

'Little Bean studied medicine with Albert,' Lund explained ponderously. 'The child has a gift for this ancient art.'

'I had to see you off,' said Albert to his former pupil. 'The rabbits you helped cure also insisted on coming. I'm sorry I couldn't help you in court as much as I'd have liked, but at least you survived.'

'It's OK. I'm just happy to be alive,' Little Bean said.

'So, what're your plans?' Albert asked.

'I'm going on an adventure with my friends.'

He beamed at Dilah and Ankel.

'I'm glad you've found some partners in crime,' Albert said kindly. 'Go, grow up together, have many adventures.'

'Lord Lund, may I ask you a question?' Dilah said, while Little Bean and Albert talked of the future.

'Feel free to ask anything, Fox,' Lund graciously offered.

'Why do you look – I mean, compared to other rabbits – why do you look so different?' Dilah cautiously asked.

'Are you referring to my size?' Lund chuckled, and Dilah had a feeling he'd answered this question many times before. 'I'm not surprised at all that you're curious about me, Fox,' Lund continued. 'I'm no ordinary rabbit. I'm a descendant of the giant rabbit clan.'

'The giant rabbit clan?' Ankel repeated. 'I remember Grandpa mentioning them . . .'

'Yes, it's an ancient and rare species, so rare that almost no one in the world knows we exist. Our medical expertise dates back thousands of years!' Lund added proudly. 'For generations, we lived in a distant and mysterious land: the enchanted forest.'

Dilah and Ankel exchanged a confused glance. Clearly, even Ankel's grandfather hadn't spoken of this!

'I guess you've never heard of it,' Lund continued. 'Very few animals can find the enchanted forest. It's a land of hidden peace and beauty, filled with all kinds of exotic plants and rare animals, as well as some of the most precious medicinal herbs in the world. Most importantly, there are traces of magic every-where . . .'

'So your size has something to do with magic?' Dilah asked, his eyes widening.

'Yes. We giant rabbits drank from the springs of the enchanted forest for generations. We grow larger and we live longer.'

Dilah blinked. 'Cool! So . . . how old are you?'

'Oh, I can't remember exactly, but I'm at least in my forties,' Lund said casually.

'Whoa . . .' breathed Ankel. Dilah was speechless. He reckoned the normal lifespan for a rabbit was about ten years.

'Can you tell us more about the magical springs?' Dilah asked, once he'd recovered.

The big rabbit inclined his head. 'Certainly. There are nine ancient springs in the enchanted forest, filled with all sorts of magical powers – healing powers, for instance. But legend has it there's another spring hidden in some unknown corner of the enchanted forest. The source of that spring, they say, is the Milky Way itself. It's called the enchanted spring, or the spring of reincarnation. As the name suggests, any animal that has been bathed in the spring of reincarnation can be reborn as a human – and as we all know, there's nothing more tantalizing than that!' Lund's eyes glinted.

Dilah's mind was spinning. If Ulla's secret treasure provided one way to transform into a human, was the spring another way . . . or were they one and the same? Ankel caught his eye, and Dilah knew he was thinking along the same lines.

'But does the spring of reincarnation really

exist?' Dilah asked, trying not to show his excitement.

'The giant rabbit clan searched for it for many years, but by the time they left, they still hadn't found it,' Lund said. 'Personally, I think it's a legend and nothing more.'

'Why did the giant rabbit clan end up leaving the enchanted forest?' Ankel asked.

Lund's expression grew suddenly grave.

'We used to be the most prosperous species there, but we were swept up in the holy war that took place a thousand years ago. My ancestors left the enchanted forest for genera-tions to go to fight in the Arctic. Most of the giant rabbits died there, leaving behind only a small fraction. Our numbers have never recov-ered, and now, we're almost extinct . . .' Lund let out a long sigh.

'A holy war in the Arctic a thousand years ago . . .' Ankel mumbled to himself. 'So Grandpa was right!'

'What're you talking about?' Dilah asked.

'When Grandpa was studying ancient animal civilizations, he said a war was the only theory that could explain the sudden decline of animal civilizations in the north,' Ankel said. He turned to the giant rabbit. 'Lord Lund, why didn't the giant rabbits return to their homeland after the war?'

'Unfortunately, its location is so hidden that they weren't able to find their way home.' Lund sniffed.

'I'm so sorry about what happened to your species, Lord Lund,' Dilah said gently.

'You're very kind, Fox.' Lund wiped away his tears, twitched his nose and smiled broadly. 'It's getting late. Time for you adventurers to hit the road!'

Little Bean and Albert had finished saying their goodbyes, as had the other rabbits gathered on the clan boundary. Now the old grey rabbit turned to Dilah. 'Fox, regardless of where you go, Little Bean is a good child – please take care of him.'

'Of course,' Dilah said gravely. 'I'll do my very best.'

'Take care!' all the rabbits called, bidding them farewell.

Dilah, Ankel and Little Bean started on their journey. The group of well-wishers watched their figures grow smaller and smaller, until they disappeared between two glossy green hills.

CHAPTER 10

Alsace

The three friends trotted along the golden path, still leading south from the rabbit clan's territory.

'So, it's probably about time I asked,' Little Bean piped up. 'Where are we actually going?'

'We're on a quest!' Dilah said enthusiastically, remembering they hadn't yet explained the purpose of their adventure to their new friend. 'See this package around my neck?'

'Yeah . . . ?'

Between them, Ankel and Dilah filled Little

Bean in on the details of the moonstone and Ulla's secret treasure, and brought him up to date on everything that had happened. By the time they'd finished their epic story, the rolling hills were fading into the distance behind them. A damp open plain lay ahead.

'Wow!' Little Bean exclaimed after the pair had finished. 'So that's what this is all about – becoming human.'

Dilah and Ankel exchanged a glance. 'So, Little Bean . . . do *you* want to become human?' Dilah asked.

Little Bean thought for a moment, then he nodded. 'I've heard that human medical expertise is extensive and profound. If I were really to become human, think of everyone I'd be able to cure . . .' He smiled happily at the thought. 'If I had that kind of power, I feel I could do a lot of good!'

They'd been travelling for many days, and now, the summer breeze accompanied Dilah, Ankel and Little Bean on their journey. The weather was scorching hot – the air moist and heavy.

Up ahead, a vast field stretched on and on, lined with crops of varying heights. A cluster of small earthen houses lay nearby. The sound of dogs barking drifted over the fields. Dilah hesitated, remembering the terrible time when Ankel had led him to the hunter's house to steal food, and the ferocious hound named Toby. The three friends decided to cut through a huge rapeseed field. They swam through the sea of golden flowers. Ankel sneezed, shooing away the buzzing bees.

Close by, a man had dozed off inside a tractor, his chair tipped back and feet resting on the steering wheel. When he heard the sneeze, he jerked awake and poked his head out, blinking in surprise. Dilah suppressed a nervous laugh as they hurried past, the farmer gaping. An Arctic fox, weasel, and rabbit – he'd probably never seen such an unexpected group of friends!

The sun blazed high in the sky and gradually they left the small village behind. Dilah relaxed slightly, glad to be out of sight of humans again. Winged insects flitted and hopped over the dry grass at their feet.

'Wait.' Dilah stopped, catching a familiar scent.

'What is it?' Ankel asked.

Dilah didn't answer. Instead, he walked over to some tall clumps of grass and sniffed carefully. Two pieces of dung lay in the undergrowth. Dilah felt his heart start to pound with fear.

'We need to get out of here immediately,' Dilah said, scanning their surroundings.

'Why?' Little Bean asked, puzzled.

'There are foxes around here, and more than one,' Dilah said grimly. 'It could be Carl's pack. Let's go!'

They veered off course, but every time Dilah stopped and sniffed the air, the unfamiliar fox scent lingered close, like a shadow. In fact, it grew stronger. Dilah's uneasiness grew too. He suspected there weren't only a few foxes around, but dozens, maybe more . . .

Dilah sped up, Ankel and Little Bean close at his heels. A suffocating tension fell over the group. Dilah stopped suddenly, his ears twitching – had he heard someone following, or was it simply Ankel and Little Bean? He glanced back.

His throat clenched – several large foxes were trailing close, a murderous glint in their eyes.

'D-D-Dilah!' Ankel stammered, as he spotted the foxes too.

Carl stepped out from the tall grass, followed by a number of blue Arctic foxes – and two fierce and powerful hyenas.

This time, Carl had brought extra muscle, and without Kassel, what chance did they have of slipping from his claws?

'Run!' Dilah screamed at the top of his lungs.

Dilah, Little Bean and Ankel took off as fast as their legs could carry them. Carl and his party immediately bolted after the three friends, chasing them through the rustling grass. After a while, Little Bean slowed down, panting, and the two hyenas pounced, wild with joy, ready to enjoy a long-awaited feast. Dilah came to an abrupt stop and spun around to protect the rabbit, and Ankel tripped and tumbled over as he did the same.

The two hyenas stopped in front of Dilah, taking the measure of him. Moments later, all of the foxes drew to a halt. Carl limped towards Dilah.

'Dilah, you're looking more and more like your father every day,' the white fox snarled.

'I'm having a hard time getting rid of you,' Dilah snapped back.

'You almost succeeded,' Carl growled. 'Heavy rain covered up your scent and tracks. If we hadn't caught a rabbit and questioned him, you might've gotten rid of us.'

Little Bean shivered at Dilah's side. 'What . . . ?' His voice trailed off.

'What did you do to the rabbit?' Dilah demanded, guessing Little Bean's question. 'Oh, he's right here, in a manner of speaking . . .' Carl remarked. The hyenas sniggered quietly.

Dilah frowned. 'Where?'

'Foolish cub. He's lining the bellies of my two hyenas.' Carl smirked. Without warning, Little Bean flung himself at Carl – but the fox patriarch easily dodged out of the way. Little Bean fell on the grass with a thud.

'Trying to avenge your compatriot?' Carl growled. 'Very well – we'll reunite you at once!'

One of the hyenas strutted over to Little Bean, licking his lips.

'Don't you dare touch him!' Dilah charged at the hyena.

Carl blocked Dilah's way, his piercing yellow eyes narrowed.

'You're supposed to be the patriarch, you're supposed to lead and protect us – but instead you've employed a couple of hyena thugs to do your dirty work!'

'Employed us?' The hyena turned around, a murderous tone in his low, calm voice. 'We'd never stoop so low as to work for a fox. We'd just escaped from a zoo when we met your patriarch. He promised to give Ulla's secret treasure to us so that we could become the kings of beasts!'

'You're peddling off our patron saint's treasure to some hyenas?' Dilah asked Carl, unable to hide the anger in his voice.

'That's not relevant,' Carl snapped, his eyes flicking momentarily to the blue foxes beside him. 'Explain the secret of the moonstone to me – now! How did you get it to work? How does it guide you?'

'I'd rather die than tell you!' Dilah said, gritting his teeth.

Carl smiled darkly. 'As expected – you're determined to be heroic. But the fates of your two companions are in my hands too. If you tell me, I might spare your friends from my hyenas. If you don't . . .' He flicked his tail. 'So, what's it to be, little hero? Cooperation or death?'

'Dilah, even if you tell him, he still won't let us go,' Ankel said, clearly fighting back his fear. 'Don't worry about us. Run!'

'I'll never leave you guys. As long as I have one breath left, I'll fight to protect you!' Dilah said.

'Have you quite finished?' Carl sneered. 'Dilah, for the final time—'

'Don't waste your breath,' Dilah hissed with curt finality. 'You already know the answer!'

Carl's eyes flashed. 'It's your choice. The rest of you stay out of this – I'll handle him myself!' Carl stared hard at Dilah and started circling around him slowly as the hyenas and blue foxes cleared the space around the pair. Dilah crouched, his pulse racing. He stepped carefully in his own broad circle, ensuring Carl was always facing him head-on. When Carl's back was to the sun, the light shining directly into Dilah's eyes, the patriarch lunged. His twisted leg didn't slow him down, but Dilah deftly jumped back, avoiding the snap of Carl's jaws by a whisker. As soon as he landed, Dilah launched a counter-attack – but Carl was quick enough to lurch out of the way before he'd even regained his balance. Dilah heard a faint whimper of pain as the older fox landed on his bad leg.

Dilah and Carl faced off once more. Carl heavily favoured one side, his hind leg clearly causing him pain – Dilah could see the tightness around his eyes, his clenched jaw. But the patriarch was heavily muscled and his teeth were sharp as he bared them in a growl. Dilah couldn't help but admire Carl's determination, fighting experience and quicker reflexes . . . but his leg was a great weakness and Dilah knew he had to exploit it.

This time, Dilah attacked first, lunging sideways at Carl's weak leg. Carl dodged out of the way with obvious effort. Dilah spun around, his tail flicking the dry grass, and rushed at the patriarch – all in one breath. Carl stumbled but didn't fall. He snapped out wildly but missed. Dilah slunk behind him and closed his jaws on Carl's weak leg. The instant Dilah's fangs touched his leg bone, Carl howled in pain and he snapped at Dilah's back, his teeth nipping a scruff of fur before Dilah jumped backwards, out of reach. At once, Dilah charged again. Unable to stand on his injured leg, Carl lost his balance and fell. Before he could get back up, Dilah had him pinned to the ground.

'Wonderful!' Carl said, gasping as he lay pressed to the ground. Dilah's mind was buzzing – he hadn't realized how strong and fast he'd grown over the months of travel. He pressed Carl in place against the dry earth. 'You're now as strong as your father,' Carl continued, 'and I hate you just as much as I hated him. You'll end up just like him too – dead at my bidding!'

Dilah frowned. 'A hunter killed my father. What's that got to do with you?'

Carl laughed softly. 'Ignorant cub! It was my doing! *I* led the hunter to your parents – and *I* led your parents to the hunter's gun. I had my vengeance for the leg your father stole from me,' the patriarch snarled.

Carl's words lit a fire in Dilah's heart, blood rushing to his head. He felt dizzy and his whole body trembled with shock. The dark grief of his parents' death rushed over him, the memory of his mother's cold body, the frozen earth in which he'd buried her. And here, beneath his paws, was the one responsible.

The world shrank: Dilah felt as if he and Carl were the only beings alive. He imagined himself biting down on Carl's throat and bared his teeth in anticipation. Soon, he'd avenge his father's murder, and repay the torture that his mother had suffered before her own death.

'What're you waiting for?' Carl snarled. 'Don't you want to kill me, Dilah?'

'Watch out!' Ankel's voice pierced the stillness.

But the warning was too late: Dilah was knocked to the ground so hard that he felt suffocated, the wind knocked from his lungs. He tried to stand but the two hyenas had pinned him to the ground. He felt the moon-stone lying heavy against his chest.

Carl stumbled to his feet, careful to keep his twisted leg from touching the ground.

He turned to inspect the limb, then glowered at Dilah. 'Do you know how much humiliation this leg has brought me? What I've lost because of it? Do you know how painful it was for me to follow you all the way here? And it's all your father's fault! The least you can do, before you die, is to tell me the secret of the moonstone.'

Dilah slowly opened his eyes. He felt dazed. The glare of the sun was extremely bright and the air was sticky. The ground . . . it was shaking. He frowned. A series of odd sounds reached his ears – footsteps? Breathing? He felt the pressure on his neck lessen. The two hyenas had heard it too.

The noise grew louder, and suddenly fox after fox emerged from the grass in all directions – but they weren't white or blue like the Arctic foxes; they were grey or red. Some were all grey, others had red backs and white bellies, others even had tails ringed with beautiful markings. Carl spun around, his body tense, clearly taken by surprise. The Arctic foxes shrank inwards, surrounding their leader – Ankel and Little Bean were released, hurrying to Dilah's side.

There must've been a hundred foxes surrounding the group.

'You are trespassing on our land,' an icy voice called out from above. Another fox stepped into view and Dilah was surprised to see that he was as white as snow. He was perched on top of a nearby hillock, his eyes blazing with anger as he peered down on the gathered foxes like a hawk. He had an authoritative air. As he caught sight of Carl, his eyes widened.

'Carl? What a pleasant surprise . . .' The white fox ran down the hill, the others shifting from his path.

'Alsace? You're – you're still alive?' Carl blinked.

Dilah looked back and forth between the two foxes, confused. Alsace – that was his older brother's name, the brother who'd left home before Dilah was born. It couldn't be him . . . could it? And if it was, how did he know Carl?

He tried to call out, but the hyenas' claws pinched his body as they pressed him into the ground. He couldn't breathe deep enough to speak.

'Yes, I am alive. I gather you're disappointed? As you can see, not only did I not die, but I'm doing just fine,' Alsace said coldly, standing face to face with Carl.

His gaze flicked over the Arctic foxes and Dilah thought he glimpsed pain flashing in his bright-blue eyes, the exact shade of Dilah's. 'Arctic foxes . . . you remind me of home.'

Alsace paused for a moment, shut his eyes,

appeared to gather his thoughts. When he opened them, he addressed all the assembled foxes – red, blue, grey and white.

'Years ago, the Arctic foxes' legendary treasure – the moonstone – suddenly disappeared, along with the great hero Blizzard. Another great hero, Gale, was seriously injured, leaving him permanently damaged, and strangely enough, it happened the very day that Blizzard went missing.'

Dilah's heart was pounding. He remembered the last story his mother had told him as she died, her words drifting back through his memory . . . *Mama will tell you another story, one I know you've never heard. This one's about two great heroes among us Arctic foxes: the story of Gale and Blizzard.* Why had she told him that story, and why was Alsace continuing it now?

'Everyone suspected that Gale had killed Blizzard and stolen the moonstone for himself. So Gale's followers turned against him. The disgraced fox disappeared into thin air. No one knew where he was hiding. He secretly built up his strength. Soon, he returned – more powerful than ever.'

Alsace fixed his eyes on Carl.

'He was determined to find the moonstone – and he knew exactly who had it: Blizzard. He had never been killed in the first place. He had fled into hiding with the moonstone after besting Gale in the fight that had injured him.' He paused for effect. 'Blizzard was my father and Gale . . . Gale is Carl.'

Dilah blinked, surprised to find tears in his eyes, his heart aching. He remembered what his mother had said of Blizzard: *He was strong, brave, calm . . . Mama will always remember his charming smile . . .* Blizzard had been his father.

'Gale – or Carl – tried to force me to reveal where my father was hiding,' Alsace continued. 'When I wouldn't tell him, he expelled me from the Arctic fox clan and told me I could never return to the north. I was forced to leave my home, to endure hunger, cold and loneliness. At several points during my long journey, I almost died. And you, Carl, will pay for your crimes with your life.'

'I didn't come here today to reminisce about the old days,' Carl growled.

'Shouldn't you be begging me for your life?' Alsace said, his voice low and calm. 'Can't you see you're overpowered?'

Carl was silent.

'Who would've thought that the legendary hero Gale, who once ruled the Arctic and made his enemies tremble with fear, would become this useless old waste,' Alsace said, his voice as cold as frost. 'And yet you've found the moon-stone, haven't you? Now you're searching for the legendary treasure.'

Carl simply narrowed his eyes at Alsace.

'I'll take that as a yes. Give me the moon-stone,' the younger fox commanded.

The red and grey foxes inched closer to Carl's group, but the Arctic foxes surrounded their leader in a tight defensive circle.

Alsace addressed the blue foxes in a calm and gentle voice. 'How many of your companions have died along the way? You've been exiled for so long – don't you miss home? The life of every single fox is extremely precious to me.

You're not the ones I want to kill. Step aside.'

'Whoever dares to betray me,' Carl barked at the Arctic foxes, 'don't forget that the lives of your families hang in the balance. You know what'll happen if I don't return alive!'

Alsace spoke in a low, threatening voice. 'In that case, all of you foxes listen: kill this waste of fur. Whoever dares to help him will die.' The circle of red and grey foxes moved closer.

'Tell them to back off, or I'll kill your little brother!' Carl said, walking over to Dilah.

'My little brother?' Alsace asked incredulously, his cold blue eyes falling on Dilah, who was still pinned to the ground by the hyenas.

Dilah managed to release a whisper of a reply: 'Yes. Dilah . . .' He met his brother's gaze.

At that moment, Dilah was sure he'd be saved. There was no way his elder brother would let him die. *I can't wait to get to know Alsace! We'll work together to defeat Carl and avenge Papa!* At this thought, his heart lit up with hope.

'Then do it. If you're going to kill him, make it fast,' Alsace said coldly. At once, a bucket of ice water was dumped on the hope in Dilah's heart. He couldn't believe what he'd just heard.

'What? You don't even care whether your own brother lives or dies?' Even Carl sounded surprised. Then, his gaze hardened. 'Well then, watch as I rip out his throat!'

Dilah was trapped and unmoving under the paws of the hyenas.

'You can't kill him!' A small voice rang out. 'He's the only one who knows the secret of the moonstone – if you kill him, you'll never find Ulla's treasure!' Ankel stepped forward, wringing his small paws.

Alsace slowly walked towards Carl, completely unconcerned about his threat to Dilah's life, or Ankel's warning. Suddenly, he shot forwards. *Thump* – Carl was thrown back, his three good legs trailing on the ground. He landed hard on his side, clearly winded. Alsace studied Carl where he lay, his eyes glinting with the thrill of revenge.

'I should have killed you when I had the chance,' Carl growled. 'Blake, Warren – if you want the treasure, you're going to have to fight for it.'

In a heartbeat, the two hyenas released Dilah and lunged at Alsace in tandem. Alsace dodged aside, barked a command, and the foxes behind him rushed forward. The Arctic foxes joined the fray, attempting to break a path through to escape. Chaos erupted inside the circle.

'Ankel! Little Bean!' Dilah kept his two friends close, ready to protect them if necessary.

After a furious fight, Carl and the Arctic foxes broke from the others, running off into the low dry grass. The two hyenas followed. It was over so fast: the battlefield stained with blood and tufts of fur. Two Arctic foxes were dead and several of Alsace's foxes lay on the ground, gravely injured or dying.

'Send some foxes to track them,' Alsace said to a grey fox at his side. 'Keep me posted on his every move,' he instructed. 'I expect this won't be the last we see of him: he won't give up on the moonstone.'

'Your wish is my command,' replied the grey fox.

At last, Alsace walked over to Dilah, his face expressionless.

Dilah's heart was filled with disappointment and fear as he looked at the cold-eyed stranger who was supposed to be his brother. He was Dilah's last living blood relative, but Alsace didn't seem to care whether Dilah lived or died.

'Are you really Dilah?' Alsace asked, fixing Dilah with a frosty stare, his gaze falling on the leather parcel on Dilah's chest.

Dilah kept silent, his heart simmering with something like anger.

'Are you really Dilah?' Alsace asked again, twice as loudly as before, as if he thought Dilah might be deaf or stupid.

'Yes,' Dilah briskly replied.

'Answer me: how are Mama and Papa?' Alsace asked.

Dilah blinked. 'Dead,' he replied softly.

'How?'

'Killed by a hunter, but Carl lured them to their death,' Dilah responded, watching for a hint of grief. Alsace's reaction, however, completely chilled his heart.

'So before they died, did they give you the moonstone?' Alsace asked coolly.

'Why do you care more about the moonstone than the fact our parents are dead?' Dilah asked, unable to keep the anger from his voice.

'Care about our parents? Did they ever care about me? Did they treat me like their child? Were they there for me in my most difficult time, when I needed them most? They gave the moonstone to you, not me! They knew I'd been driven out of the Arctic Circle but did nothing to find me! They're not my parents any more!' Alsace snapped, his eyes full of hate.

'They didn't know you'd been kicked out of the Arctic!' Dilah protested. 'They thought you'd left!'

'There's no way Papa didn't know! Do you really think he stopped paying attention to the Arctic fox clan after he went into hiding? Do you think Blizzard's loyal followers would have forgotten him?'

'They gave you life – how can you hate them?' Dilah asked. He tried to soften his voice. 'I also left the Arctic, so I can understand how you feel, but—'

'Ha! You understand? You can imagine the feeling of being driven out of your home by your own compatriots? You can imagine what it's like to trudge through mountains and rivers to get here? You can imagine the price I paid to rise from Arctic outcast to king of my own fox clan? No, I think not. Because while I was doing all that, you were the darling little apple of our parents' eyes. You can never understand the suffering I've gone through!' Alsace roared, baring two sharp fangs.

Dilah was speechless.

'Enough of this. It's time for me to claim what is rightfully mine. Hand over the moonstone,'

Alsace demanded.

'What do you want it for?'

'To be king of the animals. To attack the Arctic fox clan and exact my revenge on Carl and all of those who forced me into exile. What else?'

Dilah shivered. 'You're just like Carl – you're both controlled by hate and greed. I'll never let you find the treasure!'

Alsace didn't reply. 'Get the parcel off him,' he said to the foxes at his side.

Several foxes surrounded Dilah and yanked the moonstone package from his neck. At their leader's nod, they unwrapped it carefully on the dry grass. Alsace approached the moonstone, blue rays of light flickering in his eyes. 'This is it . . . at last.'

'Patriarch, there are markings on the leather,' one of the foxes said.

Alsace glared up at Dilah, who was quivering with rage. 'What does it mean? Does it have something to do with the secret of the moon-stone?'

'I don't know,' he lied, gritting his teeth.

'I'll ask you again: what does this writing mean?' Alsace angrily asked.

'I don't know!' Dilah insisted.

'My patience is limited, little brother. As soon as I give the word, you and your friends will be smashed into smithereens.'

'Then kill me now!' The anger in Dilah's heart flared with fresh heat. 'Perhaps killing me will let you feel you're even with our parents!'

'Lock them up!' Alsace said. Foxes surrounded the three friends, Little Bean yelping as a red fox grinned at him hungrily. 'Dilah, I'm giving you three days to think things over. If you don't tell me on the first day, I'll kill the weasel. If you don't tell me on the second day, I'll kill the rabbit. If you don't tell me on the third day, then it'll be your turn.'

'You're right: you're really not my brother – I could never have a brother like you,' Dilah said. His eyes stung. He could never have imagined that his own brother would resort to such vicious threats.

'You, follow me – and bring the moonstone.' Alsace avoided Dilah's gaze, then turned around and left.

A red fox bowed his head and carried the moonstone away – the last legacy of Dilah's mother, the treasure he had carried for months and months, guiding him on his adventure.

It felt as if his heart was breaking.

The inside of the cave in which Dilah, Little Bean and Ankel were imprisoned was lit by a sliver of white moonlight. From outside they could hear the chirps of crickets and the guard fox's muffled snores.

'Is this where our adventure ends?' Dilah said, staring glumly at the stars framed in the cave's mouth.

Ankel's nose twitched thoughtfully. After a while, he replied in a soft voice. 'Even if it is, Dilah, I'm glad I came along.'

Little Bean nodded, his ears flopping in the semi-darkness. 'I'm glad too.'

Dilah blinked in surprise. 'Really, Little Bean? We've done nothing but cause trouble for you. We've lost you your home and put your life in danger.' He turned to Ankel. 'That goes for you too, actually. If it weren't for me, you'd be safe, at home with your mum.'

Little Bean replied first. 'It doesn't matter. For the first time, I have friends – and I'd pay any price for that.'

'I agree,' said Ankel. 'I've found independence and courage with you, Dilah. I wouldn't change what happened for the world.'

Dilah was quiet for a while, an unexpected warmth spreading through his heart. He'd been unable to follow the moonstone to the end of its path. He had lost his parents and failed to find a true brother. But he'd gained so much too. All of his adventures flashed through his head – the horror and the joy, the sorrow, the excitement – the bonds forged and the friends left behind on the way. The space against his chest where the moonstone had hung felt empty, but his heart was full. He lay down and curled his tail around his paws, his friends close on either side of him.

After a while, Dilah's ears twitched. He heard the far-off pitter-patter of footsteps, drawing closer and closer, passing by the guard, and finally stopping at the mouth of the cave.

A young female fox stood in the moonlight. She had a long, pointed nose, a slender red body and white belly, and a large tail that was almost as long as the rest of her. Her eyes shone.

Dilah had a feeling his adventure wasn't over just yet.

To be continued . . .

Buona's Story

Long ago, in the frozen north, the rabbit kingdom of the Volkerkin was under threat from a neighbouring pack of wolves. The rabbit king paid tribute to the leader of the wolves to keep his hungry pack at bay. But one year, the harvest failed and the king had no choice but to offer another valuable tribute. The pack would only accept one other gift: the king's beautiful daughter.

Reluctantly, the king sent off his princess to the wolf pack . . . but she never arrived. The rabbits blamed the wolves and the wolves blamed the rabbits, sparking a declaration of war. To this day, no one knows what became of the princess. In the battle that followed, the rabbit army was decimated and the king fled with his remaining family.

All was lost until a rabbit called Buona arrived to join the king's party. Buona was no ordinary rabbit: she had fur of the purest white, like the moon. She was clever too, and she taught the rabbits to dig burrows in the earth, protecting them from the wolves. That's why, to this day, rabbits live underground.

Buona knew the burrows wouldn't be enough – the rabbits would have to venture out for food, leaving them exposed to the wolves' attacks. One night, she ran out in front of the wolf army and her white fur glowed in the moonlight, drawing the wolves into a chase. She led them towards a raging river and leapt in. Unthinking, focused on the hunt, the wolves followed. The current washed Buona and the wolf army away. She had sacrificed herself to save the rabbits.

The moon goddess had watched what happened and, in admiration, took the white rabbit's soul to the moon. From there, Buona still watches over her species and is revered by the rabbits as a saint.

But for the animal kingdoms, the battle between the wolves and rabbits was only the start. The Holy War was coming, and soon animal civilization itself would be torn apart . . .

A Note from the Author

This book is a fantastic adventure story about dreams, friendship, growing up, and life. I set out to write a story exploring the differences and connections between animals and humans, rediscovering humans from an animal's perspective and demonstrating the impact that human actions can have on animals.

The book's inspiration stems from a marvellous experience in my childhood. When I was five years old, one moonlit night, I awoke from a deep sleep and noticed a tall, milk-white figure near my bedroom window. It was human-shaped, but it had two fox-like pointed ears. Its body emitted a silver glow, and it stood with its back to me, remaining motionless . . . The following day, I told this story to my parents, teachers and classmates, but no one believed me. They thought it was just a dream or a hallucination – some people even thought I was lying. But I remained confident in what I'd seen with my own eyes, and that white shadow had made a deep impression on me. Since then, I've often asked myself, what on earth was that? Why did it come to me? Was some mysterious force summoning me? Was I a white fox in a past life? Inspired by this experience, sixteen years later, I began writing a story about a white fox who dreams of becoming human, and that milk-white figure became the model for Ulla, the patron saint of the white foxes.

I wrote *White Fox* on and off over the course of six years. The book was so long that I ended up splitting it into two books. This book only tells the first half of the story; the second half will be published next year. While writing this book, I reread many literary works and mythological tales from around the world, drawing inspiration from them as I crafted my own unique story. It was an extremely long process filled with both pain and joy. My mood would change according to what was happening to the characters, my mind expanding as they experienced various trials and tribulations.

I'd like to express special thanks to the internationally renowned publisher Barry Cunningham, the original publisher of the *Harry Potter* series and the Managing Director of Chicken House, for purchasing the English language rights to the *White Fox* series and helping to bring Dilah's story out of China and into the rest of the world. Thank you to Kesia Lupo, the editor of this book, for her numerous invaluable suggestions and painstaking effort in revising the manuscript. Thank you to my American translator, Jennifer Feeley, for using beautiful, lyrical language to reinterpret my work. Thank you to my agents at Andrew Nurnberg Associates International Ltd: Jackie

Huang, Sandra Hu and Charlotte Seymour. I'd also like to thank Ms Wang Ruiqin of the People's Literature Publishing House and editor of the *Harry Potter* series in China for helping me to turn my dream of writing into a reality and giving me the courage to embark on this path.

There are inevitably some omissions in this book, and each reader will interpret the story from a different perspective, so I don't expect it to be for everyone, but when I write, I try my best to make the story fulfilling, interesting and engaging. I hope that this story will make my dear readers feel happy, excited or moved.

This book may be over, but Dilah's story has not ended yet. This book foreshadows much of what is yet to come, and there are many mysteries left unsolved. The adventures of Dilah and his friends continue on. The secret of the moonstone has only been half revealed, and the mystery surrounding Ulla's treasure has yet to be unveiled. I promise you that the rest of the story is full of twists and turns. There are even more magical elements, more interesting characters and wonderful scenes, and more heart-stopping adventures!

Finally, I'd like to dedicate this book to fellow lovers of fantasy and adventure.

CHEN JIATONG
BEIJING, 2019